WATCHING TV WITH THE RED CHINESE

LUKE WHISNANT

Algonquin Books of Chapel Hill
1992

It has been my great good fortune to have Amanda Urban as my agent and Shannon Ravenel, Première Danseuse, as my editor. And I'm grateful to many friends for their help with the manuscript: Terry Davis, Rust Hills, Virginia Holman, Bruce Weber, Susy Cheston, Chris Glass, Dawn Robinson, and Gena McKinley.

Published by
Algonquin Books of Chapel Hill
Post Office Box 2225
Chapel Hill, NC 27515-2225

a division of Workman Publishing Company, Inc.
708 Broadway
New York, New York 10003

Portions of this novel first appeared in *Esquire* in different form.

Library of Congress Cataloging-in-Publication Data
Whisnant, Luke.
Watching TV with the Red Chinese : a novel / Luke Whisnant.
p. cm.
"Portions of this novel first appeared in *Esquire* in different form"—T.p. verso.
ISBN 0-945575-83-1
I. Title.
PS3573.H4438W38 1992
813'.54—dc20 92-10034
CIP

10 9 8 7 6 5 4 3 2 1

First Edition

for Margaret Gragg

Fade in: a medium shot of Tzu, sitting rigidly in a black director's chair, black background. He's very handsome, by Western standards: high cheekbones, full mouth, a delicate nose, glossy jet black hair cut short and brushed straight up. Only the dark eyes and the vague tint of the skin are Oriental. He wears a stiff blue work shirt buttoned at the collar; he seems uneasy and looks often from camera to

Antigone to camera again, as if puzzled or embarrassed.

ANTIGONE
(*off-camera*)
What's your favorite thing about America?

TZU
(*Accented but grammatical English, very short quick answers throughout.*)
The people. Friendly.

ANTIGONE
(*off*)
Friendly?

TZU
Yes.

ANTIGONE
(*off*)
Like how?

TZU

(*Nods his head.*)

Nice.

Three beats. Tzu looks from left of center to camera then back to left.

ANTIGONE

(*off*)

What do you like least?

TZU

Pizza. With the little . . . anchovies?

Three beats. Tzu nods almost imperceptibly.

CUT TO

A sequence showing the three Chinese cooking in their tiny kitchen. Tzu wields a steel cleaver and chops cabbage; Chen lifts the lid from a pot of rice; Wa supervises from the doorway. This scene was obviously filmed with a hand-held camera; the ef-

fect is casual, almost home-movie. Much laughter, much clatter of steel utensils and thump of chopping block. The kitchen sounds are mixed under as the interview continues voice-over.

ANTIGONE

(*v.o.*)

Chen told me that you've been on TV before, in China. Could you tell us about that?

TZU

(*v.o.*)

For a news program once I was interviewed. Before we came here. The television was preparing a report on students who go to the United States.

ANTIGONE

(*v.o.*)

What was that like, seeing yourself on TV?

TZU

(*v.o.*)

I laughed. It was embarrassing.

ANTIGONE

(*v.o.*)

Weren't you interested to see yourself?

Chen dumps a plate of sliced pork into the wok and Wa, still smiling, begins toss-frying. The camera moves in for a close-up of the meat sizzling in hot oil.

TZU

(*v.o., rapidly*)

What really interested me was the idea. The concept of the system of television, and the image of me. I was watching an image—some particles arranged just so, on a magnetic tape, which was then transformed into electromagnetic waves, and then transmitted to televisions all over the country, which converted these waves back into light and sound and motion. . . . And also because this image of me, Tzu Ng-yun, escapes the atmosphere and goes at the speed of light into outer space. All over the universe. Tzu on TV! (*Two beats.*) Extraordinary.

ANTIGONE
(*v.o.*)
That embarrassed you?

TZU
(*v.o.*)
Ah ha ha ha ha.

With chopsticks, Wa delicately lifts a piece of meat from the hot oil, blows on it, and pops it into his mouth.

CUT TO

Credits displayed on a black background:

A FILM BY BILLY OWENS

Five beats. Dissolve to

WATCHING TV WITH THE RED CHINESE

1

Everywhere there is meaning, order, shared knowledge—if you know the code. Somehow we understand one another. Over the blaring television, the black man in our front yard cries, "Flea-flicker! Flea-flicker!," pumping a swollen brown football behind his ear, sending his small sons across the snow: they zig and zag, cut and fake over footprint trails already run, and their father, lobbing wobbly spirals, leads them just right, hits them in the hands. They know the plays; they have the moves down. We stand, Mr. Tzu and I, at his apartment window and watch them run—post patterns, down-and-outs, stop-and-go's, screens, bombs, buttonhooks, hearing their hollered cryptographs: "Cortez! Ninety-five! Red Dog! Red Dog!" The boys tumble over each other, laughing, into a dirty snowbank; the brown ball skids like a puck across the ice, and Tzu turns to me and asks, "Prease to exprain frea-fricker?"

The brilliant Red Chinese!

They are the first in our city, real Communists, straight from the mainland. On their front door (2-South, across from mine, 2-North; one floor above Carl Little and sons, 1-South) they have carefully taped a white cardboard nameplate: three lines of spidery black pictographs; then, in order of seniority, oldest to youngest:

Tzu Ng-yun
Wa Wu-shiung
Chen Li-zhong

"For the post office," Wa tells me. "So we can have mail from home." And the mail comes. In Beijing, in Guizhou and Wuhan and the desolate northern backcountry of Heilongjiang Province, their friends and family carefully copy onto rice-paper envelopes my neighbors' romanized names, the blocky English alphabet and Arabic numerals of our address. Sometimes they send packages, supplies from the other side of the world: green tea, hundred-year-old eggs, dried squid, newspapers.

I was not being ironic before, calling them the brilliant Red Chinese. It's not for nothing that they're here. These are the crack troops, the avant-garde. Picked from over eight hundred applicants, elite as astronauts, they've passed an entire year of screening: three five-hour math-and-science exams, a nine-month English refresher course, psychological profiles, two separate physicals, intensive six-week briefings—all of which culminated in the award of a People's Republic stipend for studying, at a U.S. university, Systems Science and Mathematics. SSM, they call it, to me a suggestive, vaguely sexual acronym. "Hydroelectric," Tzu explained to me once. "Power systems. Communications. Control. Radar. Like in airports."

He wants to design the ideal system. Self-generating, he says. It would be perpetual. When it was finished it would go back to where it started. Like a song that repeats itself. "Like art," Tzu says. "I would be an artist and my systems would last forever. They would not need human input."

"But then your job would be unnecessary," I say.

"Ah. I would design new systems."

Brilliant. The brilliant, esoteric, curious Red Chinese, peering brilliantly out of their grimy picture window at Little and his boys, mulling over this new bit of Americana: "Frea-fricker."

I correct the pronunciation. Flea.

"Right," Tzu says. "Frea."

Then I see he's kidding, getting me back for a stupid remark I made last week, when I complimented him on his precise enunciation. (He'd politely claimed that while the Japanese sometimes transpose their R's and L's, Chinese almost never do. Is this true?) He throws me a slow-motion wink, like a carnie come-on to a mark. Once again I've underestimated him, I've been caught condescending, and his gentle rebuke is to turn the joke back on me, so I laugh, a little late, a little shamed. "Touché," I tell him, with a slight bow. "Frea. Ha ha."

"Ha!" Tzu says delightedly. His housemates smile.

"Ha," I say. "Flea. Yes."

"A flea. A tiny insect," Tzu says, then adds a word in Mandarin, softly, at which Wa nods and Chen looks, frowning, at me.

"Insect," I say. "You know. Bug."

They consider this a moment, then—

"Volkswagen?" Chen asks.

Wa, ever the security freak: "Secret listening device? For spying, for overhear conversations?"

"To annoy," Tzu says confidently. "Like when they say, 'You bug the hell out of me.' Why do you laugh, Mitchell?"

"I *bug* your pardon?"

Chen and Wa chuckle. Tzu rolls his eyes and groans, asks for a truce. I can't help teasing them, bad puns and affectionate mockery, though my tone is mostly lost in translation. I get a kick out of putting them on, tangling them up in the sticky slips and slides of English, its multiple meanings and absurd irregular verbs. But it's all in fun; I always relent, backtrack, take pity on their poor furrowed yellow brows. "Okay. A flea is a bug, an insect. Sucks blood, lives on dogs and cats, likes to set up house in your wall-to-wall shag. They bite—"

"Yes," Tzu says politely. "*Tiaw tzao.* We have these in China. So. But this flea-flicker?"

"A flea is an insect," I say. "But a flea-flicker is a play in football, a pass pattern. Like conceptual art."

Chen and Wa lean over to watch me draw it in the windowsill dust; Tzu looks on, breathing rapidly through his nose—a sound of amusement? I exprain (oops!—sorry) the object of football, the different types of plays and their advantages, the concept of a pass pattern: set, prearranged, shared knowledge.

"It is a way to know," Chen murmurs. "So they know where to throw the ball."

He stares at me oddly out of his newly bruised eye, the brow and lid and cheekbone swollen and purple. I smile. "Been watching some football, have you, Chen?"

"I like best when they throw passes," he says.

"Me too."

Tzu gives him a sorrowful look. Wa snorts. They're losing hope. In country only three months and already Chen wears jeans and a down-filled vest, listens to pop radio, jogs. He has begun combing his hair down over his forehead. He's asked me for driving lessons. He likes pizza, hamburgers, Dr Pepper. Now, worst of all, he understands pro football.

It's just a few weeks after the election. Reagan is on the way in; Carter is headed out. Everyone I know feels wretched. How the hell could you vote for Carter? someone will ask; then the cry goes up, How the hell could you not? The Chinese offer noncommittal remarks, polite observations. Only Wa ruminates darkly about the seeming uselessness of the vote—and not specifically this vote, he makes haste to point out, but the concept of "vote" in general. Model citizens, these guys—they're on top of things, they keep up: every blessed six o'clock they're glued to the tube. "*CBS Evening News with Dan Rather,*" Tzu says, "the best." (It's been nine months now but I still miss Cronkite.) They watch quietly, absorbed, apprehensive. The news is distressing. Unemployment soars off the charts into double digits. Soviet tanks mass at the Polish border. The Gang of Four trial drags on. Fanatics trash the streets of Tehran, chanting Death to America and burning U.S. flags, spitting in the camera-lens eye of the Great Satan. There's worldwide saber-rattling, malaise and unrest in the provinces, not to mention the usual floods, fires, and famines. The Chinese have never seen such news. They come to me, worried, uneasy, suspicious. "What do you think, Mitchell?"

My name is Dexter Mitchell—Mitch to most, Dex to friends. I'm twenty-four years old, single, straight, and since I live in an ethnically mixed apartment building, I should mention as a purely descriptive detail that I'm white. White white

white. White as milk, white as new snow, pasty and white as sliced white bread. My lineage is uncertain (and here over my figurative shoulder I hear Chen's puzzled query: "Mitchell, if a man says he is from New York, does this mean that *he* lives in New York, or that his *ancestors* live there?"). My mother was English, Scotch-Irish, and German; my father, "Who-the-hell-knows?-go-ask-your-mother." In other words, I'm just another mongrel American. I was raised in the heartland, took a quick B.A. in Theater Arts from a middling-good university, and played Starving New York Artist for as long as I could stand it, until I couldn't stomach another peanut-butter sandwich or shiver through one more cold shower. After a year in off-off-off Broadway and a couple of appearances in local-market pet food commercials playing second fiddle to highly paid stunt-cats, I moved here (Cleveland) to sublet my globe-trotting cousin Bob's apartment and run lights and build sets for Mixed Company, a new repertory group funded by a surfeit of arts council money and a couple of blue-haired wives of steel barons.

Note that I mentioned my new hometown parenthetically above. Were I speaking aloud, I would pronounce it *sotto voce,* and throttle it firmly, emphatically, with cupped-hand parentheses to indicate unequivocally that the lovely old waterfront town of Cleveland is extraneous, completely unnecessary to this sentence. Cleveland, smelter of ore and refiner of oil; Cleveland, defaulter on federal and state loans; Cleveland, home of 573,822 honest American consumers: wonderful town, Cleveland, replete with possibilities and infused throughout with the vibrant sulfured air of inspired midwestern industry.

I tell my neighbors not to worry.

4

Wa and Tzu do worry, though, about Chen. Especially Wa. He fears the whorish corrupting influence of materialism, he despises Chen's innocent embrace of all things American. For Wa, the United States is in its death throes, rotting from the inside out with the cancer of capitalism. Greed, violence, injustice, wretched poverty—he catches each newscast and struggles daily through the *Plain Dealer,* clips feature stories on per capita murders, coke-addict babies, starving pensioners, frozen bag-ladies. At any moment he might strike with a stat or a reproachful anecdote. He's aggressive, with tiny dark eyes and deep-throated, sinister laughter. I've seen him practicing his moves: slow insectlike blocks and kicks, sudden explosions of breath. He could kill me, I'm sure, with a single blow. Now, looking at poor wayward Chen, he pulls off his black military-issue glasses, scrunches his face like an angry child, opens his mouth—and says nothing. Abruptly he grabs his blue Mao jacket, opens the door, nods good-bye to me as he pulls on his snow boots: "To the library. For study." Tzu, apparently exasperated with them both, disappears into the kitchen.

"Wa is angry with me," Chen says.

"He'll get over it."

Chen grins. He likes idioms. I imagine him replaying "he'll get over it" five or six times, memorizing it, filing it away. We chat a bit about the recent Sino-Vietnamese border dispute. "The Soviets are waiting to see about Reagan," Chen says. "They are expansionist, you know."

Tzu reenters, bearing tea in cartoon-character glasses. I get Roadrunner. We watch the tiny leaves turn soggy and sink like bits of paper, leaving cloudy trails through the clear water. Chen and Tzu exchange a few soft words in Chinese. And then they crank up the TV—their black-and-white Sony screaming *creature feature next channel thirteen godzilla vs mothra tiny jap elves tokyo burns death mayhem black laser beams—*

"Not to be missed," I say, and—

watch these two women fight about their laundry ground-in dirt greasy oil the coldest water detergent—

"I want to tell you again Thank You about the clothes," Tzu says. "Last weekend."

They had no idea how to use a Laundromat. They'd been washing clothes in the bathtub for weeks. Tzu had come over with a box of Tide, asking in his precise way (a) what was the significance of the name? (b) what was the difference between

Tide, Cheer, and Biz? Was it Cheer like at an athletic event? Or the kind Venerable Webster's had defined as "state of heart or mind"? Or was it more like "to applaud with shouts"? ("How to tell, Mitchell, verb or noun?") And although Biz was not listed between "bizarre" (French or English?—damn this language!) and "blab," he had a polite suspicion that it was a capitalist propaganda message about big business—"Big biz, yes, someone told me this, Mitchell, and I am confused, and also—" (c) how much was one-and-a-half cups for top-loading automatics? Of course, I said, you're on the metric system. I pulled down a measuring cup. "Ah, ah," Tzu said, eyeballing it. "One moment, please?" He returned from next door with Wa and a cartoon glass; they filled my measuring cup with water and poured it into their glass, then held it to the light, chattering excitedly, looking at the level, memorizing it: for now and forever fixed, one cup is the line just below Daffy Duck's kneecap.

You would think I'd break down in the face of such charming improvisation, make them a gift of my sixty-nine-cent plastic measuring cup, be a good neighbor. I don't. I'm not. I'd rather watch them wing it. They wing it, they wing everything: their poverty-line existence, their faded Mao jackets and crisp new white boxer shorts dripping dry on the bathroom radiator, their wobble-legged card-table desk and concrete-block bookcase approach to the Land of Plenty, their soap-scum sinked, bare-lightbulbed, no-Cuisinart kitchen, bottom-line basics—everything rigged, secondhand, cast off, and recycled. Their apartment exudes that familiar student ambiance: their kitchen-corner dust balls, the scavenged sofa, the paint-chipped baseboards like an inner-city movie set, sound track provided by their pawn-shop television with its rigged antenna (a coat hanger and aluminum foil twisted like something from a Calder scrap heap, a temporary solution effected by Wa with much muttered invective and one-syllable hissing late one dusky afternoon), and its staticky, wavering reception of capitalist commercials—

nuclear chemical savings and loan six-point-

five-percent interest compounded hourly no minimum charges no withdrawal—

"The university cashes our checks," Chen offers, nodding at the TV. "The lady in cashier. He is very nice."

"She," Tzu corrects. "She! She!"

"She! *She* is very nice."

In spoken Chinese the pronouns are ungendered. I've heard Chen make this same mistake a dozen times.

We sit for a moment without speaking.

"It is so expensive to live here," Tzu says.

"Yes."

"It costs so much. To get in debt."

"I know," I say. "My next three paychecks are already spent."

They stare at each other. "But . . . you do not have the money yet?"

"No."

"But they spend it already? Your paycheck?"

"No. I mean, I already know I have to spend it myself, on certain things. To pay bills, stuff like that."

Tzu looks confused. Chen explains it to him.

"Oh," Tzu says.

"In China, everyone makes the same pay," Chen tells me.

"Dockworkers and doctors make the same?"

Another exchange in Chinese. Then Tzu says, "A few years ago, yes. Now a doctor, he will make maybe two, three dollars more a month."

"You can make much more money here," Chen says. And suddenly I imagine him in a moment of weakness renouncing his citizenship, defecting. He'd change his name and move to California. I see him surfing, roller-skating, driving a convertible down Sunset Strip. He'd sell real estate, take up electric guitar, spend shirtless weekends flinging Frisbees. He'd consume. Visions of Chen Li-zhong dance in my head: buying jazz records, a waterbed, a trash compactor. Drinking lite beer. Sleeping around. Investing. But just as I open my mouth to make a crack about mutual funds or CDs, he presses both hands to his puffy black eye, and I stop grinning. "Money isn't everything," I say. "Besides, there's too much crime here."

"Yes," he says.

"You're safer in China."

"I know. But still you can make much more money in America."

"You *need* much more money in America," Tzu reminds him.

"There's more to buy, all right," I say, laughing.

—stainless steel construction the perfect gift at only nineteen-ninety-five order now by midnight to-night not sold in stores—

"Set! Forty-nine! Seven! Hut! Hut! Flea-flicker!"

"This is a wonderful country anyway," Chen says quietly.

We watch the tag of a sitcom rerun (sitcom rerun: think they'd understand that? shorthand, shoptalk, shared knowledge, like flea-flicker, wish-bone, shotgun formation). On the screen a blond, blowsy actress, breasts nearly falling out of her halter-dress, executes a bump and a grind, slow and exaggerated, winks at her male counterpart, purrs:

You can shake it but you just can't take *it.* The laughtrack audience howls, whoops, catcalls; I expect Tzu and Chen to be puzzled, or embarrassed, but they grin as if they understand.

At the commercial Tzu squats in front of the set to change channels. They're showing last season's highlights—Dallas vs. Atlanta. "That was a pass," Chen explains to Tzu; in slow motion the receiver falls across the goal line. I listen for Little and his sons outside, but their game has ended. Tzu switches channels again.

"Here is the program," he says excitedly, cranking up the volume.

This is why they'd asked me over—as a consultant. When they're flummoxed I interpret. I'm their tour guide, their liaison, a cultural attaché explaining the culture. Taped to their refrigerator they keep a memo, questions to ask me about America—most of them from TV. "What is this about?" Tzu asks. Chen giggles. I lean forward, squinting.

A vaguely Oriental-looking man catches arrows with his bare hands. Indians reload and fire again from behind boulders. The Oriental man talks to cowboys, a sheriff. A woman in a bonnet falls beneath two horses drawing a wagon; more Orientals fill the small screen. I have no idea what the hell's happening.

"This is on every week?"

"We think so."

"I've never seen it."

"Ah."

"Weird."

"Yes. We thought maybe you could tell us," Tzu says.

"There's a lot of strange stuff on. It's hard to keep up."

"A Chinese with cowboys," Chen says. "A western."

"Who'd have thought it," I say.

Downstairs the doorbell rings. "Suzanne," Chen says carefully, standing and smoothing his red sweater.

I'm not sure I heard right. "Suzanne?" I say stupidly. Chen nods. "You mean Suzanne Betts?"

"Yes. Suzanne Betts. We are going in her car. To the mall, for shopping."

"You did not tell me this," Tzu says angrily.

"So?"

"Ching schow zow schien gnu!" Tzu tells him. *"Hung zuh!"*

—or at least that's what it sounds like to me. Chen glares at us, grabs his jacket, closes the door gently behind him. We hear him clump down the stairs, one two three four five, pause, six seven, and then in a rush the last six as he throws open the door. And then Suzanne's husky voice drifts throatily upwards, muffled, I assume sickly, against his clean-shaven neck.

Sick, oh yes—heartsick and stunned, like I'd been rabbit-punched, like I'd been hit by a truck while standing on the sidewalk minding my own business—that's how I felt then, but now, looking back, all my rancor has bled off like air from a balloon. Counting the rest of that afternoon, Chen had less than two weeks to live.

"He did not even say good-bye, Mitchell," Tzu says to me.

Without shame we both move to the window and watch them navigate the salty, ice-edged sidewalk to her blue 280-Z. She has her hand in his coat pocket and their hips bump with every step.

"Son of a bitch," I whisper.

They climb into the car—Suzanne prancing around to the passenger side, holding Chen's door for him with a mock curtsy—and drive off. Tzu is looking at my pass pattern sketched in the windowsill dust. "Flea-flicker," he says sadly.

An interception, I think, trying to get hold of myself. A turnover. Fool. Stop this pop-culture spectator-sport metaphorizing. She never loved you in the first place.

"He will not listen to me," Tzu says.

I take a deep breath. "How long has this been going on?"

"Two weeks? Before Thanksgiving?"

"Two weeks. I'll be goddamned."

"I am sorry, Mitchell. You are okay?"

Yes. I'll be okay. I slouch down on the couch, look at him and shrug, the picture of nonchalance. "Why?"

"I thought that you . . . that she was . . ." He's peering out the window.

"No," I say. "I barely know her, really."

Tzu sighs. His narrow shoulders slump.

"What would happen to him," I ask, "if he were still in China?"

"His family would be ashamed. He is counterrevolutionary. He would not be allowed to dress like that."

"That's all?"

"What more?"

"I figured they'd send him to a reeducation camp or a work farm or something."

"For wearing Western clothes?" Tzu edges onto the couch beside me.

"For becoming a 'capitalist roader.' For falling in love."

"You are a very ironic man, sometimes, Mitchell. You think people do not fall in love in China?"

"I thought romantic love was a Western concept," I mumble. Tzu looks at me disapprovingly, knitting his dark brows, but I can't stop myself. "I thought you Marxists perceived everything in economic terms."

Tzu gives a polite cough of dissent. "He likes that she has money," he says. "It is only her money. Pardon me, Mitchell, but this is a terrible country sometimes. That people should be so rich.

There are too much profits, too many things to buy. Chen is young. It confuses him."

"Wonder what her excuse is."

"Pardon?"

"Suzanne. She's one of the most confused people I know." I start to tell Tzu the gory details, then catch myself: none of my business. "I just hope Chen's careful. I hope he doesn't fall in love with her."

Tzu bites his lip, picks a piece of lint from his baggy trousers.

I sit there on the Red Chinese's green-and-brown Scotch plaid couch, with the sky outside going black and soft blue TV light washing the room. Cold tea dregs settle in the glasses. I watch wall shadows. Thinking about Suzanne. The way she brushes her hair forward with long down-strokes, bent double at the waist.

A medium shot, no sync-sound: shirtless, hair mussed, Chen peers blearily into his bathroom mirror. The camera is behind him, shooting over his shoulder into the mirror, but slightly to one side. Chen stretches his skin, pushes and pulls his smooth cheeks, pinches at his jaw. He reaches for a black-and-white can of generic shaving cream and begins to lather up. Throughout this scene we hear his voice over.

CHEN

(v.o.)

I drink tea in the morning. Sometimes some soup. An American breakfast is too big—eggs, bread. I bathe and shave.

He has run the sink full of steaming water. And as the mirror gradually fogs, Chen's reflected face slowly becomes a blur.

CHEN

(v.o.)

To shave is a good thing. It reminds me every morning who I am, and also every morning I face my face. (*Laughs.*) Good to see yourself and touch. Chen's jawbone. Chen's cheeks, Chen's chin. Ah ha ha ha.

He has cut himself. He grimaces, shakes his head no. He blots the blood with a tissue, then wipes a clear spot on the foggy mirror.

CHEN

(*v.o.*)

A young man should not wear a beard. Only old men who have achieved some wisdom, or maybe political leaders. But not young men. A mustache is also a mistake on me. (*Laughing.*) It looks ridiculous. So I shave.

ANTIGONE

(*v.o.*)

What do you shave with?

CHEN

(*v.o.*)

Gillette Trac II Razor. Different shaving creams. Throw away the razor when it is finished, when it becomes not sharp. So much American things are made to be throw away. Sometimes I look in the garbage and see so many things that could be saved, that could be used. This is new to us, this disposable products. We save in

China. Mr. Wa, he shaves with a very old razor, a razor his grandfather and his father used. And Mr. Tzu, he uses electric, because he does not like to throw away.

He has finished shaving. He bends at the waist, splashes his face, grabs a thin blue towel and hides his head in it, rubbing vigorously.

CUT TO

A montage of television shaving-products commercials, home-videotaped from broadcast, then transferred, badly, to the sixteen-millimeter master. The pictures flicker and jump; the cuts are quick—no more than two seconds on each product—as Chen speaks, voice-over.

CHEN

(*v.o.*)

This disposable surprises us, and also how many different brands there are. Just to *shave!* I remember the commercials. Gillette

Trac II. Schick. Bic. Wirl-kern-son? Remington. And electric ones, AC current. There are so many brands. And sometimes made by the same company. Why? Gillette Trac II and Gillette Good News. And the creams. Edge. Foamy. Old Spice. Nox-Eena? Too many to decide.

CUT TO

Wa with shopping basket in the A & P staring bewilderedly at an entire wall, floor to top shelf, of seemingly identical red-and-white Campbell's Soup cans.

1

Someone's heart lies broken in the snow. It's there, smashed on the edge of the parking lot, as if flung from a top-floor fire escape: a big pink heart-shaped box of chocolates, a valentine in early December. Around it fall fluted brown papers, gold foils, bonbons, and nougats scattered like a bad break on a pool table. I keep staring out through my cousin's spotless kitchen window, watching a thin winter squirrel stuff his puffy cheeks and scamper. I keep score, tally up the survivors. The garbage truck swerves to squish a few. Some are gobbled by dogs. A gang of street kids shoos the mutts away, crying with delight, Candy! Candy! They hug one another, slap high-fives, link arms, and jump like manic kangaroos, wild in the grip of a bad sugar rush. A dark-eyed girl takes up the heart's pink ribbon, brushes off the slush, folds it delicately, slides it into her pocket. She wears red galoshes, mismatched mittens. The frozen chocolates must be hard as rocks. I lean my head against the chilly windowpane and fog the view with my breath. The furnace kicks on. The dogs howl at the edge of the pavement. I'm waiting for this snow to melt.

My problem is that I've got too much time on my hands. Mixed Company is between shows—rehearsals for *Rhinoceros* start next week—and though somewhere around here there's an increasingly urgent list (*Xmas shop, groceries, Karen BD present, scour shower*), I'm just not interested. I'll do it later, whatever it is. I'm drifting. I wander from room to room, leaning against the windows and looking out at nothing; I open the fridge and stare absently: pickles, Chablis, some week-old dried-out rice caked to the bottom of a pot. "You're at loose ends," I tell the unshaven face in my bathroom mirror. The face doesn't even nod, just turns down one side of its mouth ironically.

Tzu is right: I am a very ironic guy sometimes. I'm too serious. I'm self-indulgent and cynical and maybe a little bit spoiled. I guess it's an occupational hazard that actors (even failed actors) are always watching themselves react; we're always standing off in the wings criticizing the performance. Which explains why I can't feel anything except through this veil of irony, this distance; and which is why even though I keep telling myself that my heart is broken, I know it isn't and even though I say I was in love, I know I wasn't.

When Suzanne was last here she stood bare-breasted and brazen at my bathroom mirror in a plain white pair of cotton panties, brushing her teeth with one hand on her hip. We had a flirtatious little game going, all in fun: she pretended to ignore me, and I pretended to swoon in her pearlescent presence. "You act like you've never seen a naked woman before," she chided me, so I told her I hadn't and asked if she minded; I'd only look a little. "Knock yourself out," she offered, and began brushing with great vigor and lots of elbow action each perfect tooth, mugging for the mirror while I examined with exquisite attention the lovely arch of her collarbones, the spray of freckles across her chest, the slightest droop of her full breasts, which made them imperfect and therefore even more achingly beautiful to me. I desperately wanted to take her back to bed. She caught my look, gave a frothy grin to the mirror and kept brushing.

"You know," she said, soft mouth full of toothpaste, "in another possible world we might be exactly right for each other."

She rinsed, daintily slurping water from her cupped palm; she spit, splashed more water on her face. The elastic band of her panties had rolled down over her hip; without looking she snapped it straight. The panties were white, the tiled walls white, the white floor. I was dazzled. I clutched my heart in mock breathlessness, leaned back against the wall, and slid slowly—in this, the best of all possible worlds—all the way to the base-board.

She loved it.

Suzanne Betts married young and got out fast. She's tall, buxom, broad-shouldered, healthy, has long thick red hair, freckles everywhere, strong soft hands. She wears barbaric hoop earrings and loose pullover sweaters; she slips both hands into her jeans hip pockets and leans toward you when she talks. She has golden flecks in her gray-green eyes. She winks a lot; she can whistle. She's sharp. She despises bimbos and airheads, snubs debs and dweebs, likes jocks but only to look at, and is fashionably arch with faggots (her term). She's a talented woman with a voice to match. (What does this mean? I don't know, but she says it often, with a self-deprecating little gesture: "I'm a talented woman with a voice to match.") I introduced her to my Red Chinese neighbors at a Halloween party, so you could say that this whole sorry story, this chronicle of treachery and deceit, is after all my own fault. Suzanne hovered around Chen for nearly an hour. "Most men are not mysterious," she told me once. "My life lacks mystery."

Mystery! She used to hang with a guy named Mick Czapinczyk, Zap for short, a Tristan Tzara sort who affected a neo-punk wardrobe: camouflage fatigue pants, jungle boots, Hawaiian print shirts, and cardboard 3-D glasses from the Ninth Street Cinema. They'd met at a new-wave dance club at the beginning of the summer, had drunk shooters and argued about Springsteen, whom Czapinczyk loathed and Suzanne saw as the Rock-and-Roll Savior. She wouldn't give Zap her phone number, but she did dance with him; and for the next few weeks, he pursued Suzanne across the Cleveland nightscape, from disco to theater to bistro to fern bar, contriving to arrive at each just behind her—which spooked her no end (was he tailing her around town?); but once they started dating she decided he was harmless, actually kind of sweet, and she relaxed. Zap was different—brilliant and funny, with a lot of crazed ideas; she'd never known anyone quite like him. He was working on a Ph.D. in philosophy, writing a dissertation on Theory of Possible Worlds, and after things got ugly and they broke up, Suzanne always pronounced this phrase with capital letters and a portentous pause: "Theory of Possible . . . Worlds." And she'd raise her eyebrows significantly.

I first heard this exotic locution one cold November night in Suzanne's recently renovated, ultradecadent bathroom, where we lay neck deep in bubbles in her new Jacuzzi. A digression: Suzanne's ex-husband was a contractor, and when the recession started the year before and real estate dropped, he'd picked up a Victorian cottage in East Cleveland for pocket change, gutted it, and moved in his new and lovely bride. Like much of the neighborhood, the house was decrepit—broken windowpanes, plaster lath falling out, rotten plumbing—but the joists and load-bearing walls were solid, Suzanne told me, and the first thing she wanted, before the new kitchen, before the bedroom or the den, was a state-of-the-art bathroom. They did it themselves. For six weeks they brushed their teeth in the kitchen sink, used public toilets, showered at their athletic club. On weekends they knocked out two walls and added another, plumbed and tiled and painted and sealed, and finally Suzanne had her new playroom—all chrome and tile and mirrored walls. The marriage disintegrated shortly thereafter, leaving her with this barren shell of a house—"like walking through a skeleton," she'd told me on that first tour; she'd begun to see this beautiful exterior and empty interior as some sort of ironic metaphor for her life, she said; she had the bathroom, and a bedroom with a futon on the floor and a twenty-seven-inch color TV on an heirloom credenza, and that was all. "Cultivating a minimalist aesthetic, eh?" I asked her on my first tour of the house, and she laughed, hugging herself and twirling in her empty living room.

But there was nothing minimalist about that bathtub: encased on a raised marble platform, an oversized gray six-jet Jacuzzi with a slanted back for reclining bathers. It was double-wide, and longer than usual, so Suzanne and friend could spoon side by side or lean back on opposite ends. On this particular occasion, we'd been lying lap to lap for maybe an hour, basking in the steamy candlelight. Languorously soaping my leg, Suzanne declaimed that all meaningful statements could be shown to be true or false and thus mathematically manipulable. (I've forgotten my reaction but I can't imagine it was anything more than mild interest.) "For example," she said, "take the statement, 'Suzanne is a Pisces.'"

I flicked a few drops of water at her. "You believe that stuff?"

"Yes. Pisces is a water sign. Why do you

think I take so many baths?" (Perhaps there was something to that, I thought; I'd found that it was nothing for her to spend an hour or more a day immersed in that tub.) "True or false: 'Suzanne is a Pisces.'"

"True," I said. "March nineteenth." I'm good with dates.

"Right. Now: 'Suzanne is a Libra.'"

I pretended to think.

"False, you lug," she said.

"Okay. So?"

"Well, what about a statement like, '*If* Suzanne were a Libra, she would be an air sign.'"

I couldn't even guess what she was talking about, which charmed me all the more. "Is Libra actually an air sign, whatever that means?" I asked, innocently caressing the back of her knee.

"Yes. This is not a trick question, Dex. Pay attention now. Libra is an air sign. So, '*If* Suzanne were a Libra, she'd be an air sign.' True or false?"

"Well. True."

"Nope."

"Nope? I knew it. Nope? Really?"

"Nope. An if-statement is neither true nor false. But it is meaningful. So—"

"Wait a minute. How is an if-statement neither true nor false? If you *were* a Libra, you'd be an air sign, so it seems to me that the statement is true."

"Nope," she said, taking firm and sudden hold of me beneath the bubbles; I decided it was useless to resist and from that point on began nodding my head sagely. "An if-statement has no mathematical truth value, because you can't point to a real-world example. It's all projection, speculation, see? You can't prove logically whether it's true or false. But it *is* meaningful. So . . ."

"Possible Worlds?" I asked.

Suzanne smiled, shut her eyes, agreed: "Possible Worlds."

Possible Worlds, everybody's favorite wacko subbranch of modal logic, a whole realm of theory developed just so if-conditionals and counterfactuals could have mathematical truth values, just so you can say, There is a possible world in which Suzanne is a Libra and thus is an air sign; and therefore the statement *If Suzanne were a Libra, she would be an air sign* is true. There is also a possible world in which Suzanne is a Libra but Libras are not air signs, and therefore the statement *If Suzanne were a Libra, she would be an air sign* is false. There's a possible world where Suzanne is an Aries and therefore a fire sign, and a possible world in which Suzanne remains a Pisces but all Pisces are earth signs. There are possible worlds in which Cleveland is in China, or Jimmy Carter has brown eyes instead of blue, or Ronald Reagan parts his hair on the right and not the left. In some possible worlds, Hitler marries a Jew, Caesar does not cross the Rubicon, Nixon tells no lies. An infinite number of possible worlds exist, says Suzanne, each one varying from the next in only one aspect, one if-conditional or counterfactual, and—

"Suzanne," I said, "this Czapinczyk guy has rotted your brain. This isn't philosophy. Whatever happened to metaphysics? What about God and Free Will and Being and Nothingness? What about the Great Questions?"

"In an absurd world," Suzanne said, standing, streaming water, reaching for her Donald Duck towel, "philosophy is liberated from the Great Questions."

And at the time of that conversation, early November, she'd been liberated from Czapinczyk for almost a month. She and I had been to dinner twice. We'd gone dancing. We'd taken two baths. We had slept together once. And that next morning when we walked out to her car, Czapinczyk had been there already. He'd bought a package of hot dogs and impaled each one—all ten—on her antenna. He'd left a condom dribbling fluid (milk, we decided later) stuffed up inside her door handle. And he had taped over her license plate a sheet of paper bearing in black Magic Marker the inscription "SLUT."

I'm getting ahead of myself, neglecting my chronology. All this—the languid bath, the hot-dog attack, Theory of Possible Worlds—was weeks before I found out. Everything's out of order here. I can't help it. I close my eyes, try to call up Chen's dead face, and see Tzu instead. (Which is not bigotry, the knee-jerk racist's they-all-look-alike-to-me mentality—because they *don't*—but rather a failure of memory, the flicker of concentration: the American mind's flip-flop change of channels, that toxic information-and-image overload. Cf. Wa, below.) If I seem to ramble, it's a symptom of these fragmented times, this snafued society. I can't quite keep things straight. There's all this stuff mixed and mingled. I try to remember Suzanne's smell, the warm peppery taste of her, and instead I think of the dimple in the bottom of a Bordeaux bottle, which brings back for me her breast—not because of the shape, but because she bent toward me that first night in her bed, holding the wine up to the candle, taking my hand and caressing the indentation with it: "Look. Baby tits." (Maybe you had to be there.) I get these random images, these jump-cut flashbacks, without warning. Tzu tying his shoe. Czapinczyk's black Rabbit cruising by my building. Wa weeping inconsolably at the inquest, rocking from side to side in his plastic chair. Remembrance of things past.

So I'm sifting all these moments, drifting,

sorting, looking for some place to start. Like it's a gray rainy afternoon and I've got a hundred blurry snapshots and an empty photo album: I know which pictures go together but I can't decide what to put on page one.

4

The first time I ever saw them, Tzu and Wa were struggling up the stairs with the plaid couch. Chen, baby-faced, good-natured, was directing them in a loud bemused voice when he saw me; he smiled and said hello. I thought they were deliverymen; the apartment next door to me had been vacant several months. "Someone moving in?" I asked, nodding at the couch. They had been in the States less than a week, and Chen said, "Pardon?"

I repeated myself more carefully; he called out a question to Tzu and Wa; they replied; then Tzu told me, over his shoulder, that they would live here. "In these buildings. Apartments."

I saw them again a few days later, trundling an old bicycle up our back fire escape. I was taking out the trash, so I stood aside on the landing and we went through a series of awkward, apologetic graces: After you—Please, you first—No, no, you. The extremely polite Red Chinese. "Hot out," I said stupidly, brushing by with my bag. Wa's upper lip glistened with sweat; his glasses glinted. With those clunky black specs and his badly cut hair, he looked for all the world like some Japanese kamikaze, an evil caricature from a World War II propaganda poster: short, sallow, slightly buck-toothed—the Yellow Peril incarnate. "Is it . . . ?" Chen began, then looked to the others for support. I waited, smiled encouragingly, ready for some profound query.

"Is it so hot here always?"

"Not always."

And then they had a hundred questions for me. I stood, holding my plastic bag of garbage, speaking delightedly from the top of my head. They told me their names and asked mine. They shook my hand around the garbage bag very slowly, pumping it twice as long as usual, thoughtfully, as if practicing. They were from China, I learned. Taiwan? "No, China," Wa said.

"Red China? I mean, the mainland?"

"We are Communists," Tzu said, and they all laughed at once.

"Really?" I was interested. "I've never met any real Communists before."

The word slipped from my tongue like liquid, easy, and I was horrified at once, as if I'd just said *nigger* or *kike* in mixed company, the offended parties present. But the Chinese didn't blush; perhaps they thought of me in turn as a capitalist. A running dog of capitalism, emptying his capitalistic trash.

They had just paid thirty-five dollars for this heavy, ugly, green bicycle, used, a little rusty, and

Wa wondered if they had not been cheated. I assured them after a gander at the merchandise that they had gotten a deal; they seemed astounded. "In China, a bicycle is five, six dollar," Chen said.

"And it have ten . . . wheels?" Wa added.

Wheels?

He tried it in Chinese.

"Gears!" Tzu said.

"Gears!" Wa said.

"Oh," I said, "you mean a ten-speed."

I told them to be careful, to lock the bike indoors. They knew, Tzu said: "Crime here is very bad." I told them to come over any time I could be of help. "Good-bye," Tzu said. "Good-bye," Wa said.

Chen said *'bye.*

5

I was impressed by how well they'd adjusted. Here they were in the heart of the richest, craziest, most complex nation on the planet, and they opened bank accounts and jaywalked and chatted with cashiers in the grocery checkout line, just like anyone else. "This country," one of them would say, shaking his head; the other two would laugh or sigh or nod: "America," they'd say, as if one word could explain everything, the whole gamut of their reaction. By turns they were charmed, puzzled, repulsed, elated; they were dismayed and excited and bored and confused. Sometimes they were scared. (One lazy Sunday morning Chen and Wa came to me, clearly apprehensive, to ask whether it was safe to go outside, was anything wrong, had something bad happened? They'd seen no one on the street, no pedestrians, no joggers, hardly any traffic—surely some catastrophe was afoot. Was there a curfew or a war? "Everybody's at church," I told them, "that or sleeping late.") I think they were intrigued by our ethnically mixed neighborhood—even Tzu, who had traveled all over Asia and Africa—and amazed at the wealth of their neighbors, most of whom owned color TVs and cars. They were sophisticated people, and knew better than to generalize about America based on their incomplete knowledge of our grimy little corner of Cleveland; but on the other hand, like everyone else, they were plugged into the national nervous system, the life-breath and heartbeat of their home away from home; they had *Dallas* and *60*

Minutes and *Charlie's Angels*—and the innumerable inexhaustible insistent commercials, aspirin cars deodorant cake mix floor wax Sears chewing gum tampons dishwashers lip gloss cars beer GE restaurants denture cleaners blue jeans bacon toilet bowl cleaners life insurance paper towels eyeliner McDonald's cough syrup cookies Reagan airlines hairspray bread nasal mist tires potato chips *Friday the Thirteenth* pickup trucks cold cream toilet paper—The Ten Thousand Things that have no substance, Tzu said, laughing; what was that? I asked, Chairman Mao or the *Tao Te Ching*?

They were much in demand as dinner guests, in those early weeks; as far as anyone knew, they were the first Communist Chinese ever to visit Cleveland, and that made them trendy, gave them a kind of left-wing cachet. They dined with Marxist professors and with the chancellor, with Chinese-Americans and with the mayor, and once were treated to a pizza lunch by a ladies' book club. Money was tight, so they hardly ever turned down a free meal, no matter how unpalatable they found these big hunks of meat and odd lumpy vegetables; they struggled heroically with their knives and forks and resisted with varying degrees of success the many fiendish Yankee plots to get them drunk. All three could swill the weak American beer like water, but Scotch, their drink of choice, was another story entirely, and unlucky Chen, enduring the smug taunts of his roommates, spent most of one miserable September Sunday in a rigid fetal position suffering through his first (and last, he swore) tequila hangover.

In early October Channel Three's *Cinema Classics* showed *Charlie Chan at the Wax Museum,* and my neighbors, randomly flipping channels during a study break, happened on it, then sat transfixed by this flick, seeing themselves for the first time, I suppose, through American eyes. Two hours of the Great White-suited Detective inspired in them a protracted and wacky Inscrutable Chinese kick: for weeks afterward everyone and everything was Honorable this and Venerable that, and his roommates began calling Chen "Number One Son." This was subtly funny to them, these vulgar Hollywood stereotypes; they laughed silently, with their eyes scrunched shut. They affected Charlie Chan's eloquent broken English delivery, his languid hand gestures. Apropos of nothing, they'd offer ironic aphorisms, mostly non sequiturs and an occasional pun. Unloading groceries one rainy afternoon, Tzu announced, "Dog that eat stay alive," and Chen told me in a high singsong, "Man of thousand face not shave so good." "Leave alone Honorable Acquaintance," Wa advised, "and go study for Honorable Math Exam"; and Tzu cuffed Number One Son good-naturedly: "Chop chop!"

And then it was Halloween, a holiday that caused them considerable confusion. Did Americans (such practical people!) really believe in ghosts? What was the theory behind jack-o'-lanterns ("The melon face with lights," Wa called them)? What exactly was a trick-or-treat? "Young vandals," Tzu suggested, and Chen happily announced that he was "freakin' out." I finally gave up trying to explain the Bourgeois Concept of Costume Party—surely they have something like it in China, but my guys played dumb—and told them they'd have to see it to believe it. "But we have no masks," Wa finally said. Chen wanted to go anyway. Tzu vacillated, folded his arms and flexed, hung his head to one side and thought. "Okay," he finally decided. "We go." Wa said he would not, no way, put a paper sack over his head. But somehow—threats? cajolery? fond teasing? all in Chinese—the other two convinced him. "Mitchell," Tzu asked, voice muffled, peering out from the ragged eyeholes of his brown A & P bag, "in America when you are invited to a party, you must stay until it is over?"

"It's just down the street," I assured them. "You don't have to leave with me; you can go home whenever you like."

We traipsed over to the Johnsons' under a waning half-moon. Leaves blew horizontally from eaves and skittered in the gutters; smoke streamed from chimneys. We passed a gaggle of girls dressed as disco whores, children in fishnet hose and gold chains turning tricks-or-treats from door to door, and behind me the poky Red Chinese gawked and giggled just a bit. ("You should not call us anymore the *Red* Chinese," Wa would tell me a few days later. "We are Chinese. The only Chinese. From China." Wa has the party line by heart. "There is only one China," he says. "And it will be united." I have heard him, in hot debate with several Nationalist Chinese, arrogantly list the provinces of his country: places he's traveled: Jilin, Hunan, Xizang, Taiwan . . .)

I remember feeling as we ascended the Johnsons' creaky staircase that for once, I was happy—truly and inexplicably happy. Maybe it was the moon. Or the pleasure of wearing my softest, oldest, knee-torn jeans. Or maybe the sight of the blue 280-Z parked in front. I took the last four stairs two at a time, pulled on my rubber Reagan mask, stomped and beat a drumroll on my red sweatshirt, and with a blood-chilling scream, kicked the door open like a TV cop. The Chinese hung back uncertainly, brown eyes astonished behind brown grocery bags. "Hey, Mitch," Teri said. "Nice mask." She wore a plastic pig nose herself. "Who are your friends?"

Inside was music, food, beer. People passed joints and, as always, the Johnsons' loaded and running Bell & Howell Super 8. The film of their last party flickered on the cracked plaster wall. I watched a long pan of the hors d'oeuvre table—stuffed mushrooms, a cake in the shape of a horse, chips and dips. Then a shot of Mark mock-mooning the camera, still in his underwear.

The Chinese accepted beers and slumped together on the sagging edge of a daybed, lifting the bottoms of their bags to drink. I stood by them awhile, introduced them around, encouraged them to mingle, then left them wide-eyed at Jane Ellen, a tall blonde dressed as a stalk of celery. I wandered into the darkened den, where every piece of furniture and both rugs had been crammed against one wall and a mob of monsters, ghouls, and goofs were pogoing to "Rock Lobster." The stereo volume was on six but it sounded like eleven. A hand-lettered sign above the mantle said DANCE GENTLY—OLD PEOPLE LIVING BELOW.

I nodded at a guy wearing a Khomeini mask, which wasn't as funny as it used to be—this was day 361. A drunken ballerina in a pink tutu thumbed her pretty little nose at me. "You're an asshole," she said. (Me?!) "And so is Carter. I'm voting for Anderson." I nearly pulled my mask off. A woman dressed as a hooker laughed, told the ballerina to get real. "Anderson is a joke, honey. He can't even get it up. Believe me, I know." "I'm voting for Reagan," a cowboy said. "I know he's senile but I'm sick of this Carter bullshit." I was putting on my Reagan voice, clearing my throat to say thanks, when I became aware of Czapinczyk yelling from the next room, "All the way from China!"

Wa had taken off his mask. They'd all taken off their masks, and Tzu sat to the side, touching his long graceful fingers to his face over and over in a gesture both poignant and effeminate, explaining God knows what to Billy Owens, in mufti.

"They flew from China to Pakistan!" Zap yelled.

"Yes," Wa said. A crowd was gathering.

"Pakistan to Paris!"

"Very nice, Paris airport."

"Paris to D.C.!"

"Washington: nice."

"D.C. to here!"

"Yes."

"And not one single second of jet lag! Eastern medicine, listen, their internal clocks run differently. Time is subjective! No morning after!"

"What," Chen asked, "is jet lag?"

That's when Suzanne Betts grasped my shoulders from behind and nipped the nape of my neck with her naked teeth. It gave me butterflies. "A love bite," she murmured. "Happy Halloween, Dex."

I turned and did a double take, stepped back and looked her up and down. "Wow," I said.

Suzanne was a mermaid. Crepe paper seaweed tangled in her long red hair, green glitter dusted across her arms and shoulders, green eye shadow, a green-sequined skintight tail that started two inches below her navel, and two good-sized seashells that somehow defied gravity—she was stunning. Between the shells hung a single large jingle bell on a leather thong. "You like?" she asked, and only then did I notice the pale green lipstick (where does she *shop*?) and her gold-flecked green nails. "I'm amazed," I said, and I really was. "You're usually so . . . you know . . ."

"Demure?"

"Yeah. Demure," I said, laughing.

"Well, Dex, it's Halloween. If you can't get wild on Halloween . . ." She shrugged and her bell jingled. I locked eyes with her as I carefully lifted the bell from between her breasts; she gazed back at me evenly, a little amused, I could tell, at my audacity. The bell chimed a low mellow note, like a tiny gong. "What's the story with this?" I asked.

Suzanne smiled.

"It's a fairy bell," she said. "Made by Czechoslovakian fairies, deep in the forests of darkest Czechoslovakia."

"And it's for . . . ?"

"Decoration, mostly. Enhancement. And good luck, of course. I'd ask you to dance, Dex, but I'm a bit hampered by this tail."

"I bet you are," I said, gently replacing the fairy bell. "How the hell did you drive in that getup?" and then, like a bad joke, we both said, "Very carefully."

By then someone had started the next reel of the party film. "Hey, remember this?" I asked, pointing across the room at the wall, where a twice life-sized Antigone Jackson bent, grinning, over a chocolate birthday cake; the image was dark, grainy, a little out-of-focus, and when she puckered her lips and blew, the candles flickered, flared, and then sputtered out—and as the room lights came up again, there we were in the background, five months ago. Suzanne was leaning toward me with her hands in her hip pockets, smiling; I couldn't quite tell what my expression was. Then the camera swung erratically to the floor; next: Antigone ripping into a big box wrapped with a blue bow.

"That was a great party," I said.

She smiled. "I'd totally forgotten about it."

We watched ourselves cut a silly tango in the birthday movie. The same DANCE GENTLY sign was visible on the wall behind us. After a minute or so Czapinczyk cut in, too cool in his 3-D glasses. He threw me a dismissive backhand wave and waltzed Suzanne out of the frame. Watching my film-image's apparent disinterest—*Dex shrugs, slides both hands into his pockets*—I laughed. "Well, I was *his* date, after all," Suzanne explained.

"Well, sure."

She touched my shoulder. "But we're not seeing each other anymore. For almost a month now."

"I know. I heard. Are you doing okay?"

"Yeah. I'd be great if he'd just leave me alone, stop calling and coming by and harassing me. But let's not talk about it."

"Okay."

"So, Dex." She craned her neck, stood comically on tiptoes, did an exaggerated three-sixty of the whole party. "Where's your date tonight? Didn't you bring anybody?"

"Just the Chinese bag-boys."

"Ah, so," she said, and giggled.

I've forgotten what came on the dance tape

just then—some love song popular that summer, sung hoarsely without much embellishment—but as it cranked up Suzanne grabbed my arm and told me to listen, there was a great moment coming up. "I love it right here," she said, "right when the bass kicks in, right . . . *now*"—and the bass kicked in and the speakers throbbed and she raised her slender arms to show the goosebumps: Suzanne Betts, a low-frequency person.

"I've gotta ask you something, Suzanne."

"Go for it."

"How have you got those seashells attached?"

"Very precariously."

"Seriously."

"Trade secret, babe."

"Does it hurt?"

"Hmm." She smiled sweetly and swung her thick hair back over one shoulder. Her fairy bell jingled. "Now how shall I answer that?" she said.

"Are you getting demure on me?"

"Coy, maybe," she admitted. She reached behind my mask, curled a lock of my hair around her finger and tugged gently.

Sometime later I noticed more yelling from the living room. *Abbey Road* was issuing from the stereo, and Czapinczyk seemed to be leading a gang of happy drunks, including Teri and Mark Johnson, in a chorus of "She's So Heavy." Only instead of singing "I want you," he had everyone going "I Wa Tzu, I Wa Tzu so ba-aa-aa-aaadd," pointing back and forth between the two Chinese each time their names came up, with Chen grinning delightedly between them on the daybed. I couldn't stop laughing, but Suzanne said somewhat grimly that Zap was deranged. "Introduce me to your friends," she demanded. "Then I'm taking you home."

I looked at her to be sure. "I can walk," I said; "it's just a couple blocks."

"Don't look a gift horse in the mouth, Dex. Did you ever take a bath with a mermaid?" She advanced disdainfully toward the Chinese, and I said to myself: Mitchell, you lucky boy.

It was an hour later before I could tear her away from Chen.

6

Poor Chen! He had the most charm and the best nature, and a simple, ecstatic sense of wonder about us. Every day brought something amazing and new: cheeseburger and fries, rock and roll in the supermarket, drive-thru bank windows. He was cute—no other word for it—with a round Oriental face, those too-wise epicanthic eyes, and a big, easy smile, and of the three he was by far the most malleable. Suzanne couldn't keep her hands off him, Tzu told me later. Teasing, coquettish, she was constantly sneaking up behind him to bite the back of his neck, tickling him under the arms (aspirated gasps of helpless laughter), tweaking his nipples or pinching his flat little ass through his blue jeans. I never saw her like that with anyone. She nearly cooed around him.

Oh, I'm indulgent, wry in my jealousy; my tone is equivocal, though I feel it down to the very marrow. When we met at the start of the summer, she'd just acquired her high-powered divorce attorney, a sleazeball in a three-piece suit who eventually nailed her ex for big alimony. I never got the whole story, but it seems Suzanne caught hubbie in the act with an old girlfriend and filed for divorce the next day. "The son of a bitch had been screwing her brains out all along," she told me, "and they picked up right where they left off just as soon as we got back from the honeymoon. An ugly movie." Suzanne was brokenhearted and enraged; it made her distant and gun-shy. We went out anyway, dinner and a movie, a few wet kisses on my cousin's couch—not much else. Her motto was "Love sucks, and then you die." She was so tired of being serious, she said; she just wanted to play the field, have some fun. The last thing she needed was a boyfriend. "This is a terrible cliché, Dex," she told me on our second date, "but I'm just not ready to get involved." Then she met Czapinczyk and got involved. What the hell, I told myself. It was only two dates . . . but *Mick Czapinczyk*? Who can figure? I'd see them now and then, here and there around town, Zap in his punk getup, Suzanne standing self-consciously aside; and once when they'd fought, she called me crying at 2:00 A.M. By October they were officially not speaking, though they still hung out with the same people and saw the same concerts. At the Halloween party she seemed genuinely glad to see me, but for all my flirtatious patter I was wary, wary, wary. She drove us home—to her place, I mean—where on my knees in her new bathroom I unzipped her sequined mermaid tail and left it coiled on the marble floor like the shed skin of some gorgeous snake; I held the backs of her thighs and nuzzled her belly. We took a two-hour bubble bath, kissing and stroking and soaping and squeezing, but it ended up as two hours of unconsummated foreplay—neither of us felt ready. It took two more cautious dates for us to become lovers.

I say we became lovers, but in truth we only slept together twice (Suzanne Betts, low-frequency person). Once at her place, the weekend after Halloween: we made love for hours: we lit a half-dozen candles, spilled wine on each other, and watched our shadows moving on her mauve walls; she wore an untied black silk kimono and a pair of silver hoop earrings, and she kept them on all night. We lost ourselves in each other; we banked and turned and dove and soared, we tangoed and rumbaed. We ravaged her bed. We were frantic, we were slow, we surprised each other with our gracefulness; we astonished each other and did it every way we could, and then twice again in the morning. And once at my place, a few nights later. Where it was just as good but less intense, where we used no props or costumes but kept our eyes open and watched each other the whole time. I imagined her throaty Ohs and Yeses and her other cries to vibrate into the plaster walls, to hang and ring with tension pulsing in the very wood and brick until the whole building shook and stalled with her on the edge of an imminent collapse, and then went over. Ah, Suzanne, you rocked and rolled and clutched me deep; the next morning you stood at my bathroom mirror and let me look, laughed at me looking, while I held my breath and next door in their identical bathroom Chen or Wa or Tzu (but probably Chen because of the way things worked out) opened their side of our back-to-back medicine chests and cleared his throat twice, deeply, and you grinned at me as the sound came through, Suzanne, you grinned and blew me a kiss that I see now, looking back, was just another of your good-byes.

Long shot: Wa walking on campus, blue trousers, blue jacket, carrying a cheap vinyl briefcase, presumably full of books. He strides determinedly down a sidewalk, between rows of flame maples, with an occasional yellow or red leaf drifting through the shot; he looks straight ahead, as if he's been told to ignore the camera. Sync-sound—birdsong, distant laughter, automobiles—is mixed low under Wa's voice-over.

WA

(*v.o.*)

Everyone here is very nice to me. And to Chen and Tzu. And have take time to exprain everything. Like . . . how to catch a bus, and the telephone bill, and this kinds of things. And the holidays.

Now at the end of the sidewalk, he stops to greet two young women—classmates? friends?—with Asian features. They chat a moment, then Wa, grinning, wheels and points directly to the camera. The women cover their faces, then turn their backs. Wa laughs. He throws an arm around each and drags them back into full view; after an awkward moment, they giggle and wave shyly.

CUT TO

Long, bumpy tracking shot of an enormous Thanksgiving dinner spread. Apparently another shot transferred from videotape—home-movie quality. Turkey, dressing, cranberries, sweet potatoes, corn, bowl after bowl of foodstuffs.

WA

(*v.o.*)

Thanksgiving—nice holiday. Professor Gunderson invited us, and he tells the history. I do not *pray* to give thanks but I can think of many many fortunate things, how I am fortunate man. So it is good holiday. (*Laughs.*) Mr. Chen tried very hard but he could not eat the turkey. Or the corn bread dressing.

A white American family has seated themselves around the table. They pray a long time. Then the father, in a gesture of acknowledgment much like the one the Asian girl made in the previous shot, waves to the camera, picks up a steaming bowl of green beans, jokingly offers it to the photographer.

CUT TO

Interior shot, kitchen, an hour or so later: two women washing dishes, backs to camera. The refrigerator door swings shut and a teenaged girl comes into view; she's apparently putting food away. The camera begins a slow forward tracking shot, through the kitchen door, into the dining room, past the table still cluttered with serving bowls and wineglasses, through the den alcove to where the men and boys sprawl on couches and big throw pillows in front of the Thanksgiving Day football games. The camera tracks slowly straight up to the TV, closer and closer until the shot degrades into indiscernible blurs of color and motion.

7

Billy Owens's first film was a precocious no-sound no-budget paean to loins and legs, shot on sixteen-millimeter video for his community college TV-production class. He called it *Shorts,* and at four minutes thirty-seven seconds there wasn't much to it: just a couple dozen below-the-belt vignettes of human figures wearing various styles of short pants—cutoffs, khakis, culottes, Bermudas, black biker spandex, tacky pastel madras. There were no faces, no torsos; the legs held forth in a mishmash montage: white and brown and black thighs and knees standing still, walking, posing, dancing, running in place, riding exercise bikes, karate-kicking, roller-skating across the frame—fat legs, hairy legs, long smooth women's legs, Antigone's slender coffee-colored legs, Billy's father's fishbelly white legs, his mother's legs road-mapped with blue and purple varicose veins. ("I helped do that," Billy said once, pointing. "My mom was pregnant six times. That's what carrying a half-dozen kids will do to your legs.") Billy's buddies mostly claimed to like the film, though truth be told no one really knew what to make of it. Was it art? Was it satire? Was it a goof, just a jumble of images? Coy Bill wasn't telling; he'd shrug or frown or hack his ugly chuff-chuff laugh, and say that whatever *Shorts* was, it hadn't impressed his instructor much. She was a former New York daytime-TV assistant director who didn't care for Billy's Cleveland boy genius routine: she told him his movie was derivative to the point of plagiarism, a cheap imitation of Yoko

Ono and early Warhol. She derided his use of the fixed camera, took off points for the lack of sound track, and gave him a D for not following the assignment (make a commercial for a local business). So Billy's second film, *The Eloquent Instrument,* featured both sync-sound and a cluttered array of self-conscious camera angles, including a fairly intricate (if a bit bumpy) tracking shot. He was shooting telephones: the film was a loose arrangement of scenes of people phoning in orders for pizzas, dialing radio talk shows, and calling 800-numbers for income-tax assistance; there was even some hokey footage of my cousin (Hi, Bob!) smashing a phone with an ax. "One thing I learned doing this piece," Billy said later, "is that I can't direct for shit. I'm useless with people. But in making this film I found my subject matter: objects, technology that we take for granted. I don't give a damn about shooting people except as they relate to the technology I'm filming." (*Au contraire,* Bilbo: the best bit in your whole silly movie is that lovingly photographed scene in which Antigone's six-year-old sister, a button-nosed moll with enormous black eyes, dials a number for live phone sex to ask where babies come from.) Billy spliced together innumerable shots of the thing itself: the basic black desk phone, the light blue princess, the wall-mount white, the rotary pay phone, the antique crank-box, the Mickey Mouse headset, phone after phone after phone ringing, buzzing, chirping, beeping, wailing off the hook—"I wanted to sound-track her to death," he said, talking about his instructor. He handed it in with a haughty smile and a typed two-page manifesto explaining his aims and aesthetics. A week later *The Eloquent Instrument* came back marked C minus (*Does not follow assignment!! See me!!!*) and in disgust Billy dropped the course. He'd been wasting his time, he said, to think that a TV class could teach him anything serious about film; TV was video, and video was garbage. He bought 4,000 feet of sixteen-millimeter raw stock, rented a cantankerous Arriflex, and went looking for his next movie. For a few weeks he and Antigone scrambled around town in her old brown Rambler, working on a piece about gasoline pumps, but he couldn't find anyone to interview except a nutty old man with wild white eyebrows who collected and restored antique service-station paraphernalia; no one seemed to give a damn about gas pumps. Billy trashed that idea and was unhappily driving all over Ohio filming water towers at sunrise, an unfocused project that he dropped like a shot when he hooked up with my neighbors. It took him two weeks of cajolery and reassurances, but somehow he convinced the three Chinese that he only needed a couple hours of their time, it wouldn't be any trouble at all, and this movie would foster good relations between our two countries; and the instant they reluctantly agreed, he started shooting, using a thousand-dollar arts council grant (originally awarded for *Gas Pumps*) and a corner of his living room rigged as a soundstage (background draped black, black director's chair).

I'd never cared for Billy Owens. I didn't like his arrogant talk and his snooty affectations, or the way he absently shook his finger at you as he pontificated on art and life and the importance of film. (He had a way of making the simplest ideas sound unnecessarily profound.) I didn't like his work, which seemed cold and impersonal—and not in a deliberate stylistic way, but rather out of lack of vision. I didn't like his pale shiny face or his struggling-artiste wardrobe, his navy peacoat and his shapeless black beret. I especially didn't care for the solicitous way he patronized Antigone (on whom I had developed a secret, innocent, and playful crush), mocking much of what she said with a condescending pat on her small brown hand and rubbing her short dreadlocks absently, as if she were some little black troll doll. And yet she loved him! And they were getting married! "As soon as we finish the film," Billy announced as he popped open a beer at my kitchen table, and Antigone giggled and told me she'd understand if I were too heartbroken to come to the wedding.

This was sometime in late September, I think—maybe the first week of October. I congratulated them, told Antigone my heart *was* broken but that time heals everything, then asked when the film would be finished.

Billy shrugged. "Who knows?" Antigone said.

"How's it going?" I asked, tilting my chair back.

"Hampered as usual by piece-of-shit gear and limited resources," Billy said, "plus I don't yet know if any of the footage is going to cohere, whether it'll have anything intelligible to say or just be an arrangement of random moments." He began some monologue about Godard and jump cuts and the fractured mosaic, but Antigone cut him off with a quick flick of her hand. "This film," she said, "it's just like all your other films: we gonna make it or break it in the cutting room." She looked at him lovingly. "You don't ever know what you're trying to say 'til you start putting it together anyway."

"Well, yeah," Billy said. "If it's a question of montage versus mise-en-scène, I'll go for the montage every time. A sixteen-millimeter Arriflex and a Sony editing machine—Billy Owens's Shape Your Own Reality kit."

"Are you guys really getting married?" I

asked softly, but Billy didn't even blink. "We're not chained to any deadlines. We're improvising around these restrictions. I'm a technique freak—you can solve anything with enough technique. Like using voice-over narration. I've got a lot of footage with real low-quality audio—like all the location shots, anything that I didn't shoot on the soundstage, all the outdoors sequences—"

"The sound sucks," Antigone explained.

"If I'd had the gear and the personnel, I could have done sync-sound. But I don't, and the sound is problematic as is, so I've been interviewing them, no camera, just tape"—he tapped his Sony with hand-held mike—"for the v.o. stuff; and anything that's good, I'll just lay it right over the action footage."

"How are *they*?" I asked, inclining my head toward the wall, through which we could hear the muffled chopping of Chinese dinner being prepared.

Billy shrugged again; his beret slid sideways but he caught it and nonchalantly pushed it back in place. Antigone said, "Wa walked off the set the other day. We hit some kinda nerve, I think. I was asking him about TV, and he went off, man, wild, yelling in Chinese. No telling what he was saying."

"I kept rolling," Billy said, "just in case it was good. I think I can get Kimi Hu to do a voice-over translation."

"Or maybe Chen or Tzu would do it," I suggested.

"Good idea," Billy said. He pulled out a blue ballpoint, started writing on the back of an envelope.

"I'm still amazed that they'd agree to let somebody make a film about them."

"Well, yeah, that's the thing," Antigone said, "and Billy, you know I don't feel so good about misleading them this way—see, we told them that we were making a film about TV, and that we were gonna interview about a hundred people, and that we might not even use their footage in the final cut. That's why they didn't worry about talking to us. But the truth is, this film *is* about them, and they don't even know it."

"It's not about them," Billy said. "It's about TV."

"It's about them watching TV," Antigone corrected him. "Tell the truth, Billy Owens."

For the first time since I'd met him I saw Billy blush. He pushed his envelope across the table to me. In careful block letters he had printed the words WATCHING TV WITH THE RED CHINESE. "That's our new title."

"Catchy," I said.

"I hate it," Antigone said. "You gonna have the Chinese government suing your ass, Billy. Sic their evil Fu Manchu attorneys on you."

"Yeah, but—" Billy stopped in mid-gesture, finger lifted toward Antigone. "Hey, check this out. I just noticed this." He retrieved the envelope from me and with a flourish circled the first two letters of his title: WA. "And look at *this!*" He circled the CHIN in CHINESE.

Antigone began laughing, bopping him fondly on the top of the head with her flat palm. "What about Tzu," she teased. "Whatcha gonna do 'bout Tzu? Change his name to 'TV'?"

Without a word I took the pen from Billy's hand, pulled the envelope back over, and circled the NG in WATCHING. "Ng," I said, an impossible sound in English, so I tried it again: "Ng. Tzu's first name."

Billy went wild with delight. He hugged Antigone, insisted on slapping me a high-five. And though he still irked me, with his pretentious talk and his arrogance, I let loose and laughed along; and it must have been then, in that moment of forced giddiness and good feeling, that I decided Billy Owens wasn't so bad: I didn't have the heart to tell him *Chen* was spelled with an E.

8

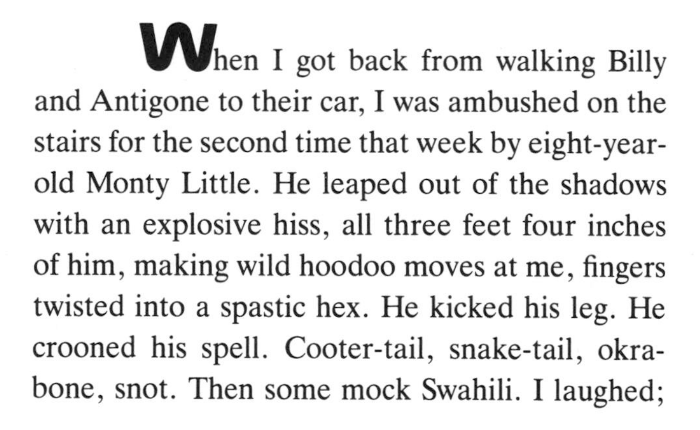

When I got back from walking Billy and Antigone to their car, I was ambushed on the stairs for the second time that week by eight-year-old Monty Little. He leaped out of the shadows with an explosive hiss, all three feet four inches of him, making wild hoodoo moves at me, fingers twisted into a spastic hex. He kicked his leg. He crooned his spell. Cooter-tail, snake-tail, okra-bone, snot. Then some mock Swahili. I laughed;

we'd been playing this little game for a few weeks and I admired his bizarre touches. "That four-eyed Chinese man is scareda me," he said, " 'cause I'm black. They don't have no brothers in his hometown. He's skunk-funked."

"Well, I'm not," I said. "How 'bout letting me by, voodoo chile."

"I'll put a bad mojo onya."

"I'll put one on you, chap, if you don't cool out." I raised my left hand, fingers splayed, and crossed my eyes and contorted my face horribly. Monty seemed unimpressed. "I seen you with that black lady," he said accusingly as his brother Cortez banged through the front door with a yelp.

Cortez wasn't much older than Monty—a little over a year, I think—but he stood several inches taller; and where Monty was roly-poly, with a round little tummy and fat baby cheeks, his brother had lanky limbs and a lean, almost haggard look. Today he wore a clear plastic head-cover, like a shower cap, to protect his Jheri-curls. "What is that thing, your do-rag?" I asked him innocently, but he just brushed me off.

"Who y'all talking about?" he demanded.

Monty stuck out his tongue. I raised my eyebrows, turned up my palms: beats me.

"Just a minute ago!" Monty yelled. "That black lady. Out in the parking lot with her hair up in dreadlocks."

"Oh, man! That ain't no black *lady,*" said Cortez, thrusting his lewd little hips. He clutched at his heart. "That's a stone *fox*."

"Who?" I said.

"He knows," Monty said. "Look at him grinnin'."

"You know who," Cortez said. "Over here all the time. Drives a old brown car. She got a funny name," said Cortez Little.

"Yeah, that's her," Monty said, "Antifreeze or something."

"You are so dumb, Monty," Cortez said disgustedly.

"Antigone," I said, trying not to laugh. "It's Greek, a heroine in a Greek play"—and that really confused them: a black woman from Greece who used heroin?—but I didn't stop for questions.

"We're just friends. There's nothing going on. Besides, she never comes here alone; she's always with her boyfriend."

"Yeah, it's a poor homely white boy," Monty said. "I been witching him too."

"Stupid," Cortez muttered. He glared at his brother.

"I scared that Chinese man. Made him wet his pants!"

It looked like a standoff. I made a move for the stairs but Monty was too quick for me. He drew himself up with arms spread, banister to wall. "Let me by, Monty."

"Cooter, okra, snake-tail, skunk," he chanted, eyes crossed.

"Come on," I said. "I got things to do."

"White man, black man, Chinese man."

Without warning Cortez jumped between us, saying in a low furious voice that he'd knock Monty upside the head. Monty came out of his trance and raised his fists: "You try it."

"Stomp you right thu the floor."

"Try it."

"Baby. You a pussy."

"You mama."

"You don't even know who your mama *is*! You don't even *have* a damn mama."

Their father swung open the front door to hear Cortez screaming at me the story of Monty's sorry origin: "The *po*lice finds him in the gutter. And brings him up to our door and lights is flashin' and they give him to Dad. Born in the sewer, where the shit and pee is."

Then Cortez suddenly found himself jerked into the air, hoisted upward by one arm until he was staring terrified into the scowling face of his father.

"Dad! Don't, Dad!"

"Cortez, I don't *ever* want to hear you say that about your brother again. Not for any reason, not any time. You got that?"

"But Dad—"

"Got it?"

Cortez nodded. Little let go and he dropped lightly like a cat. His brother blew him a big raspberry.

"And Monty, just what do you think you're doing?"

He looked fiercely at the floor, thought, kicked at the stairs. Finally he came up with an answer: "Nothing."

"He was hexin' Dexter!" Cortez cried. His father bent his finger back and told him to call me Mr. Mitchell.

"I don't mind," I said.

"I do," Little told me. "They have to learn respect."

Little taught Social Studies at the junior high school around the corner, and he knew his stuff. He was working intermittently on his M.A. thesis in American History; his director had him tracing folkloric elements of eighteenth-century slave narratives, but what Little really wanted to write about was Indians. "Cheyenne, preferably," he told me once; "I had a great-great-grandfather who lived briefly with the Cheyenne after the Civil War." He was an intense, elegant man with gold-rimmed glasses and precisely clipped diction, thin and long-limbed like Cortez, and glancing from one to another there in the stairway I couldn't help wondering whether Monty really was adopted, and what had become of the boys' mother (or mothers); then Monty made a furtive twisted face at his brother, and Cortez retaliated by tattling: "Dad, Monty's been spooking them Chinks."

Little darkened. "Cortez, I want you to cut this trash talk. Speak grammatically. You sound like street urchins, both of you."

"Cortez is a dirty liar," Monty said with great dignity, hands on his hips. "I have not done nothing to them."

"You the liar," Cortez said, going for him.

Little had to break it up. He sent Monty outside and Cortez to his room. "Young hellions."

"They're good kids," I told him.

"I don't know where they get it," Little said. "I don't talk like that."

"It's the vernacular."

"Ignorant, is what it is. It makes them sound ignorant. I didn't raise them to speak that way. They pick it up at school, I guess."

He invited me with a dip of his head into his sandalwood-scented, cluttered apartment, where black and red pillows were strewn across the floor and a swirl of reggae throbbed from the stereo. "How about a beer, sport? Make yourself at home." He disappeared into the kitchen but kept popping his head out to ask about my cousin: How did he like Nigeria? Where was he headed next? When was he coming home? "He's got two more continents to go," I called over the music, "and I think he'll keep going 'til his money runs out." Little whistled admiringly. "A grand tour, eh? That's the way to do it," he said, reappearing to hand me a frosted mug. I perched on the paisley sofa and took a sip: Heineken. The reggae tune pulsed and pumped and then faded out slowly. I drank more beer. Little took off his glasses and rubbed the bridge of his nose. "Nigeria," he murmured, shaking his head. "Yep," I said, "Nigeria." "Umm," he said. We gazed dumbly at each other, then both laughed and looked away. And that was the first time I saw it: in plain view on the end table by his battered blue armchair, a blue-gray snub-nosed Remington .38-caliber revolver. Which the police would later confiscate and hold as State Evidence Exhibit A.

Medium shot: Chen sitting in the ladder-back chair in his apartment bedroom. He wears a blue work shirt, open at the throat, over a red T-shirt. He's looking slightly left of center at Antigone, off-camera, as she reads the titles of his books.

CHEN

Most of these I have borrowed. From American friends.

ANTIGONE

(*off*)

The Adventures of Huckleberry Finn?

CHEN

Yes. By Mark Twain.

ANTIGONE

(*off*)

Why?

CHEN

I want to read something American. To understand America. So I told this to my neighbor, Mr. Dexter Mitchell, and he said this book was the best American book. And that it would be easy to read for me. (*He smiles a little sheepishly.*) I could not read it very much, though. The boy that tells the story—Huck Finn—did not go to school, so his English is very bad. Maybe as bad as mine? (*Good-natured laughter.*) So I could not read it. Too much look up every word, and many words that are not in my dictionary.

ANTIGONE
(*off*)
Did you like what you read?

CHEN
Oh yes, very much.

He looks at the camera, nods, smiles uncomfortably. Looks back at Antigone.

ANTIGONE
(*off*)
How about *Hamlet*?

CHEN
Yes. The same problem. Too much vocabulary. Is it English? Very hard to understand. I know the story but I can't read it. And it

is not American anyway. Hamlet was Denmark. And Shakespeare. A great writer but not American.

ANTIGONE
(*off*)
The Autobiography of Malcolm X?

CHEN
Yes. Good book.

ANTIGONE
(*off*)
Why?

CHEN
This book was loaned to me by my neighbor downstairs. Mr. Little.

CUT TO

Little, being interviewed in his big blue armchair.

LITTLE

He was down here one day saying he wanted to read something about America, something quintessentially American. Of course, that's my phrase—that's me putting words in his mouth, you might say—but that's pretty much what he wanted. The guy upstairs had loaned him *Huck Finn* and told him that was the fundamental American book. I told him—ah, let's see—I think I said that opinion was a little one-sided—

CUT TO

CHEN

He said it was bullshit.

CUT TO

LITTLE

(*with a half-shrug*)

I mean, it's been a lot of years since I read that book, but Jim is hardly a representative black character. He's pretty much Uncle Tom'd out, eh? And that book is what, a hundred years old? I thought Chen might prefer something a little more recent, a little more representative of how things are now. Plus I knew that being a Communist, he would be interested in some of Malcolm's views, the sociological stuff, the economic basis for racism, et cetera.

CUT TO

CHEN
(*groping*)
I think that I could understand, maybe? Malcolm X?

ANTIGONE
Relate to him?

CHEN
Relate to him. Yes. Better than Huck Finn.

ANTIGONE

Why is that?

CHEN

Ah . . . He is black in the white culture. Outside. And I . . . (*He turns both palms up with a charming little smile.*) You see. Like Malcolm X. And also, he did not speak good English. Again like me. He could talk to criminals and other black people but he could not make a good impression to white people. But then when he was in prison, he teached himself to write English with the dictionary. When he was in prison, every day he would read in the dictionary, and he learned new words. So I have to try to follow this example and read in the dictionary. (*He pauses, looks up, bites the side of his lower lip* [exactly like Suzanne!].) I learned also many words from reading this autobiography. Like the word "conk"—

ANTIGONE

(*off-camera, breaks out laughing and can't stop*)

CHEN

—and also "homeboy." Is this not right?

CUT TO

LITTLE

The problem with his idea is that there's not a quintessentially American book anymore, just like there's not a quintessentially American history or a quintessentially American art, because there's not a quintessential American experience anymore. There's no sense of continuity anymore, and there might never have been but it seems like there used to be. At one time, even we blacks shared the white American experience—outside of it, of course; it was unobtainable, but at least it was real and we knew what it was. But now nobody knows what it is. This is a culture in decay, a culture in fragments. It's fragmenting more and more every day, even among the subcultures. There's fifteen or twenty different value systems out there now. So of course there's no American novel anymore, no American book. There's no shared reality at all nowadays, with the possible exception of—

CUT TO

ANTIGONE
(*off*)
Television.

CHEN
(*nodding, smiling happily*)
Yes.

ANTIGONE
(*off*)
Tell us about television.

CHEN

I have been thinking about television very much. I watch TV in my free time and sometimes even when I am reading. And I talk about TV with Wa. This is a new experience for us, to have so much TV, and so we want to understand it.

CUT TO

WA

(*sitting against the black background, arms folded*)

We have television in China. But it is not commercial. It is information and curtular *[cultural]* programs. And not so many people have TV set in their house. More in public places, to watch as a group. So nobody watches like here in America, six, seven, eight hours a day. Or all day long.

CUT TO

CHEN

One night I watch the news. Local news, terrible story of a double murder, right here in Cleveland. Just near this neighborhood. Then I watch the *CBS Evening News with Dan Rather,* to see the election race about Reagan and Jimmy Carter and John Anderson, and also to see if there is anything about China. Then some game shows. Tzu and I laugh at them because of the people who play. Spin this or guess this and win money, or a car, or . . . steak knives? (*Laughs.*) So I am going to turn it off but then a funny show comes on. So I watch. And then I go to turn it off but I try the other channels to see what might be on, and something good is on so I watch it, I don't remember what. And then *M*A*S*H* is on. Good. And then more and more and then the news is on. I have watch all night! Night is over! A waste.

CUT TO

Medium shot: perched on a red plastic milk crate in their living room, their black-and-white TV tuned to a football game, screen flickering in that familiar strobe of television being filmed. The announcers and the crowd are barely audible as Chen continues to speak, voice over.

CHEN

(*v.o.*)

When I am watching football, I think about how everyone else in America is also watching. So many million people watching the *Monday Night Football.* Seeing the same plays and hearing the same words. Seeing the same commercials. Men drinking beer. In bars with the TV on loud. At home. Or at their friends' house. Or at the airport or in stores where they sell TV. Because I have seen this—people in the stores, shopping, stop to look at TV. Or people on the phone, talking to each other, watching the game and talking about it on the phone. Or even in their cars, people watching in their cars, on little TVs. And I think what this is like, to have the whole country watching, to have everyone together, a system, a series, parts that relate to be a whole thing. They are connect. . . . And to me this is very American. This is America, more than books.

He nods twice, looks at the camera. Two beats.

ANTIGONE

(*v.o.*)

Thank you.

CHEN

Okay?

9

Billy's film was not exactly a documentary. He took certain liberties. He had no compunctions about staging shots, suggesting settings (Tzu and Chen at McDonald's), and supplying props (Wa holding a Frisbee); nor did he balk at drafting friends and family as gofers or to do cameos. For several weeks I'd successfully evaded his attempts to interview me about the Red Chinese, pleading camera shyness or lack of interest or plain ignorance where my neighbors were concerned; but when Billy found out that Chen wanted American driving lessons, he was indefatigable. "You have to do it, Mitchell," he insisted. "It's not an interview. You won't have to say a word. I just need some action footage—something outdoors, moving—or the film will stagnate. You can't say no." Which was how I found myself in the Kmart parking lot one mid-October Sunday morning, standing with Chen beside my gray Toyota and glaring into Billy's Arriflex. "How do you feel, Mitch?" Antigone yelled, pointing the boom mike like a bazooka; I just shrugged and turned my back. "Be a sport," Billy said. "Get in the car, Chen," I muttered.

Billy got plenty of footage. First he filmed Chen struggling with his shoulder belt. Then a close-up sequence of Chen starting and killing the engine a half-dozen times. Then a head-on series of clutch-popping lurches and stalls, filmed at considerable risk and maximum obnoxiousness through the windshield. Then a shot of me getting out of the car, advancing threateningly, waving a rolled-up newspaper like a lug wrench and yelling incoherently. Then a long shot, from across the parking lot, of the little gray Toyota creeping out into three lanes of eastbound traffic.

10

"I know how to steer," Chen told me, after we'd shaken Billy and Antigone, "and to go and stop. But the gears are hard." So I found myself foolishly explaining as best I could the transaxle, the drive shaft, the concept of the sticking point—to Chen, whose undergraduate degree was in mechanical engineering, and who spoke three languages to my one (Tzu spoke *four*—French and Russian besides the obvious two), and who could probably disassemble a Soviet-built carburetor blindfolded and calculate compression ratios in his sleep. Should they survive the Big Nuke, Chen & Co. and a few others of their ilk could rebuild civilization down to the last toaster oven with just a few ball bearings and a good library. And I was teaching him Intro to Auto Transmission?

He picked it up quickly. And I realized that he must have spent some time behind the wheel in China, because within an hour of easing onto the bypass, Chen seemed at home, smiling at himself in the rearview mirror. At green lights he politely tapped the horn behind daydreaming drivers. He flipped the turn signal with his little finger, nonchalant, and nodded to people he passed. He punched radio buttons without looking. "Next you'll be wanting to cruise the drive-thru at McDonald's," I said.

"Big Mac Attack," Chen mumbled; he scraped a tire on the curb and laughed. "Sorry!"

"It's paid for," I said, a concept that confused him so thoroughly he ran a red light.

"Now see, Mitchell," he said grinning. "You will make me get killed."

We were coasting through a bombed-out neighborhood — boarded-up storefronts, overturned trash cans—and Chen seemed to hit every pothole. "How was your date with Kimi Hu?" I asked him.

A mischievous look came into his eye. "Kimi Who?"

"Kimi Hu."

"Who?"

"Ha ha," I said, and Chen sputtered with laughter. "My next date," he giggled, "is with Kimi What."

"Take a left here," I said. "Careful, there's a cop—"

"I see it. And then Kimi Where."

"Ha ha. So how did the date go?"

"Good. We went for a movie, and then ice cream." He reached over to crank up the radio: an oldie: the Beatles doing "Revolution." "I like this," Chen said. "Good beat. Lennon, Mc-

Cartney. Everyone knows the Beatles," he said, catching my look of surprise. "In China too."

"But not this song?"

"Why?"

"Listen." I twisted the volume up another notch, just in time for the last bit of the third verse: the part about Chairman Mao. "All riiiight!" I sang.

Chen laughed, plainly confused. I turned down the radio and quoted the lines slowly. He shrugged. "What does it mean—make it with anyone?"

"It's a line for Wa," I explained. "And other people like him. It means you shouldn't be blinded by ideology—Communist or capitalist. You'll turn everyone off."

Chen seemed to think about that as he tried to shift into third and grinded into first by mistake. I winced. "Sorry!" He nearly took a right, the wrong way down a one-way street, and then circled the block aimlessly. We needed to get back—the after-church traffic was cranking up—and I directed him across two sets of railroad tracks ("Always look both ways! Both!") and through an alley to the service road, then a right and down the ramp under low gray clouds, merging onto Interstate 90. Blinker on, pedal floored, don't stop, they'll let you in, they have to let you in, don't stop—then suddenly we were wedged bumper to bumper between two tractor trailers, drivers cursing, headlights flashing, air horns blaring to wake the dead, and it looked for a few seconds like we weren't going to make it; Chen's pale face stared straight ahead, his eyes widened and his hands went rigid on the steering wheel, and without looking over he asked me out of the side of his mouth, "Mitchell, do you believe in God?"

11

In the few months that I knew him, Chen and I spoke only this once about God. When he'd finally wedged my poor little Toyo into a tight parking space and jerked the brake all the way up with both hands, he triumphantly tossed me my keys and insisted I come up for a cold glass of his favorite American soft drink, Zup. He was confused, he said, that anyone with any intelligence could believe in God; yet more than once in class he'd heard Professor Gunderson quote Einstein (whom Chen seemed to revere second only to Mao) that "God does not play at dice." (I wondered briefly whether there were dice in China, and if not, exactly how that remark would translate.) Chen was a scientific determinist: his cosmology allowed no room for free will. He took the macroview and believed with Einstein that in four-dimensional space-time, future events are determinantly present (that is, they exist already); and he was an acolyte of the newly developed science of chaos, which perceived the mathematical beauty and logic of randomness within systems—the microscopic flowering of crystals, the lazy up-spiral of cigarette smoke in dead air, the minute flutter of a butterfly's wings in Belgium that ends up as a snowstorm in Beijing; but he could not reconcile himself to the idea of a Supreme Being, an anthropomorphic deity who set up the system's ground rules. Einstein's apparent belief in God as causal agent troubled Chen no end.

I was tired, stressed out, and frayed from bad traffic vibes, and wanted to go home. I drained the dregs of my Zup (7UP, I'd discovered; look at the logo) and stood up. "What you're talking about is science, Chen. What I'm talking about is people, and people have to believe that there's free will. We want to believe that things could be otherwise, that there are other possibilities. I don't like thinking that everything is predetermined, whether by God or by some kind of mathematical theorem. Human beings need to believe they have choices."

"Mitchell," Chen said carefully, "everything that happens to you, everything that you think you are deciding, it is because of logical pattern, some set of laws, a mathematical function. Nothing is chance! You are only too close to see it, you cannot step out of the system to see the system work, but if you could—"

Just then, with the precise timing of a bad sitcom, Tzu burst from his bedroom, waved his *Hammond World Atlas* at us, and asked in a voice of exasperated fury, "Mitchell, where is Bum Fuck Egypt?"

In November the weather got serious, as they tell me it always does in Cleveland. We get the arctic jet stream here, howling south for half a hundred unobstructed miles across Lake Erie, and then not even the smelting of ore and vulcanizing of rubber and all the hot caustic smoke of our daily industrial sweat can keep this ugly city warm. Normally November flows by with a steady and gradual acceleration, but this year, the month belonged to Ronald Reagan, and it passed in starts and fits, lurching forward, double-clutching, dragging, then picking up speed as it fell through the calendar: the frantic opening week, all last-minute bombast and late-night election returns; the ice-pack-on-the-head hangover of the second week, letdown and exhaustion and slow sobering; the blink-of-an-eye third week, with Thanksgiving popping up suddenly like a grinning tin turkey in a shooting gallery; and then the month might as well have been over, bring on December. Looking back on it now, I find that my November blurred by like a bunch of Billy's bad jump cuts, and all I have left are quick-take flashes—tech rehearsals, shows and cast parties, and a few freakish phrases from Czapinczyk's odd-hour phone calls (he'd been harassing me regularly ever since I'd left the Halloween party with a certain mermaid). Suzanne and I had our several tentative dates, our dinners and baths and at last our two sleep-overs, and then for eight nights straight I was tied up running tech crew on *Six Characters in Search of an Author* and didn't see her at all. We met for lunch the next week but couldn't get our schedules right for the weekend; and then I headed off on my eleven-day end-of-show Thanksgiving break, which I spent in Cincinnati with Mom and Dad and my sister. ("So, Dexter, are you dating anyone?" "Geez, Mom—give Dex a break!" "He doesn't need a break—he needs a girlfriend. Is it serious, honey?" Maybe, I told her, but I didn't really know.) I got back in town the last hour of the month, just in time to drive Chen to the hospital.

He'd been walking home from campus, a late night at the lab, and he got jumped—mugged, assaulted, whatever you want to call it—right there on Euclid Avenue, on the sidewalk, under a streetlight, in plain view. He hadn't resisted. If he had been with Wa, they could have fought them, he told me later, because Wa was a good fighter; but he was alone. Somehow he'd dragged himself home, where he'd found me unloading my car in our dark parking lot, road-weary and unaccountably wistful, wondering if 11:04 on a Sunday night was too late to call Suzanne.

We sat a long time, well past 2:00 A.M., in the

emergency room of St. Vincent's—or more accurately, the ER waiting room, which could have passed for a fairly nice bus terminal in some cities: scuffed gray tile floor; a ceiling-mount TV playing a *Benson* rerun; molded plastic seats, fuchsia and sick green, bolted to the floor. The receptionist had taken Chen's name and insurance number (policy provided by the People's Republic of China via the university's International Student Health Office) and had apologetically informed us that he probably needed X rays but "it might be a while." Even through the pain of two bruised ribs, a split lower lip, and a rapidly blackening eye, Chen could see his injuries were minor compared to the carnage around us. It had been a while since I'd spent Sunday night in a public hospital ER, and I felt a little queasy. We'd walked in just as they'd started unloading a two-car head-on collision—two fatalities and a stoic little girl with a compound fracture of the femur, sitting upright on her stretcher. A man with both wrists slashed wandered in; he stood dreamily by the admissions window blinking at Chen, who blinked back, horrified; they couldn't stop staring at each other. Finally the man fainted. There was a ten minute lull; then they began wheeling in the gunshot wounds (the worst of which was a woman who'd taken a shotgun blast in the pelvis) and the drug O.D.s—some catatonic, some tripping and screaming on the citywide PCP craze. We watched a Hispanic boy rhythmically slamming his bloodied head against the men's-room doorjamb and saw a black man fling himself at a black policewoman, raking his long fingernails down her face, cursing her for a whore. A white security guard clubbed him senseless. He lay on the grimy floor in front of us, lifted his head to Chen, and muttered, "Black police showing off for the white cop"; then he vomited. Chen shuddered. He whispered something in Chinese, twisting his blood-caked lip into a careful grimace. I looked at his pallid face, his tightly closed eyes, and wondered if he were in shock, if he were bleeding internally. Then I realized he'd been freaking—a twitch, a shiver, an involuntary recoil—every time a black person walked by.

Because they'd been black, the men who mugged him. That's just how it happened. They could just as easily have been white, or Hispanic, or even Asian (Koreans, Vietnamese boat people). In our neighborhood, they could have been Lebanese or even Russian Orthodox Jews, recent émigrés sponsored by the local synagogue. But they weren't. They were black, both of them, and in the space of a few horrible moments, innocent Chen, who had never even seen a non-Oriental until he was in college, felt for the first time the full weight of black anger—these men hated him!—and with his goodwill in shreds around his feet he must have realized how pathetically naïve and superficial his identification with Malcolm X was, how meaningless. He was outside the white culture, yes, but these people didn't give a damn about that; they regarded him not as ally but as enemy and despised him because he was the wrong color. It had nothing to do with money or need. This was race. From that moment on, Chen radiated an almost palpable racial fear.

"They were black men, you know," Chen told the police, and when pressed for details, all he could provide was "One tall. One not so tall." The difficulties of telling the unfamiliar Caucasians apart were nothing compared to these mysterious Negroes. He could of course distinguish them by size or haircut or some identifying item of apparel, like sunglasses or a gold chain necklace, but beyond that, even the basics of black physiognomy were beyond him, and after the mugging the whole dark race must have merged for him into a single indistinguishable threat.

They had, after all, offered to kill him. They'd pushed him up against a brick wall at the edge of an alley; one nicked his neck with a jagged piece of green glass; the other held a broken brick to his head and threatened to bash his brains out. ("Splatter?" Chen wondered later. "Smash?" What exactly had been said? He was obsessed with remembering the precise terminology, trying to understand, as if interpreting the act would control it, defuse it.) When they opened his wallet they found no credit cards, no useable ID, and two dollars. "Two dollars! What you thinking, coming down here with two dollars," the tall man said, smashing the brick into the wall beside Chen's head; bits of clay and mortar ricocheted off and grazed the man's cheek, which only infuriated him further. "We oughta kill you *dead,* motherfucker," Chen said they said, "for two goddamn dollars. Shit." Then they hit him twice in the face, knocked him down, and kicked him hard in the ribs. "Welcome to America, gook," one said.

"Carry some cash next time. Don't leave home without it."

As mugging stories go, this was pretty standard stuff, just your basic street-corner petty theft, assault and battery, nothing special. Anyone in town could tell of worse—someone they knew or the friend of a friend or, God forbid, they themselves had been beaten, raped, shot from pure meanness ("She gave him the purse and he stabbed her anyway"). Chen himself had heard these cautionary tales, I'm sure, along with all the attendant advice and conventional wisdom about sticking to well-lit streets and offering no resistance. But nothing you hear or read or see on TV ever prepares you, really, for a cocked pistol poked in your face or the point of a razor held delicately under your earlobe. Chen was never the same afterwards.

The doctor who appraised his X rays was white, a third-year resident on a bad night: two fingers of a bloody rubber glove protruded absently from his rumpled OR scrub suit, and his wire-rimmed glasses were lightly flecked with blood, which he seemed not to notice. He perfunctorily ran his hands along the patient's side, complimented him on his incipient black eye ("That's gonna be a helluva shiner"), and announced that the orderly would tape Chen up. The orderly in question stood six-four, weighed perhaps two-twenty, and was black as night. Chen, who had suffered without comment the ministrations of the black X-ray technician and a blood-pressure/thermometer/pulse exam with a black nurse, balked here. He totally lost it. He recoiled, yelled my name (I was standing in the doorway), then tried to swing at the orderly, which hurt his ribs so badly he almost passed out. "He will not touch me," Chen kept saying, and after the doctor got the idea and sent both me and the orderly out I could still hear Chen's hysterical voice muffled by the closed door.

Two months later, at the inquest, Suzanne Betts would claim it was this young doctor who advised Chen to buy a gun. (Wa and Tzu both said it was Mick Czapinczyk who suggested it; Zap of course denied this.) Suzanne said that when the doctor heard Chen's story, and found out his address, he cursed the university—what idiots!—and said that they should issue handguns at registration if they planned to let poor foreign students, who couldn't know any better, live in such a war zone. He told Chen that the city was overrun by dope—most muggers were hopped up on coke or angel dust and they probably *would* kill him next time—and that he himself never went anywhere unarmed; to prove it he pulled a sleek silvery automatic from a hip holster and waved it before Chen's disbelieving eyes. Or so Suzanne says. Somehow I can't visualize it. It's just too incongruous an image: an ER physician packing a pistol through a ward full of gunshot victims. Chen must have thought he was dreaming, trapped half-asleep and helpless in some nightmare America.

On the way home we stopped at a twenty-four-hour Walgreen's for antibiotics and codeine. Chen was already sedated (they'd shot him full of Demerol after he freaked) and several times he reached over to pat my hand as I shifted gears. "Thank you, Mitchell," he murmured, peering at me with slit eyes. He looked eerie and stoned in the green dashboard light. "My good American friend. Thank you." I told him to lie back and take it easy, we'd be home in a few minutes. He closed his eyes, said a few sentences in Chinese, then added, "Okay?" "Okay," I said firmly. "Good," Chen said. "Please do not tell him." "Him who?" I asked. "*Her,*" he said. "Not tell her." "Okay," I said; "her who?" But by then he had passed out, groggy head against the window, and I had no idea whom he could have meant. It would be another three days before I'd find out about him and Suzanne.

Close-up of Kimi Hu, a pretty, petite Chinese-American woman, twenty years old. Her silver ear-rings jangle as she speaks.

ANTIGONE
(*off*)
You dated one of the Chinese guys?

KIMI HU

I don't know if you'd call it a date. I went out with one of them, Chen. Well, yeah, it was a date, I guess. Pizza Hut, *Star Wars*—dinner and a movie, a real American date.

ANTIGONE

(*off*)

So how was it?

KIMI HU

Fine. You know. Nothing special, really. (*Pause.*) No sparks.

ANTIGONE

(*off*)

Think you'll go out again?

KIMI HU

Probably not. He's nice and everything, but a little boring. Plus he's a chauvinist. I mean, maybe that's pretty bad to say, but it's true. I've never met a Chinese man who wasn't. Especially men from the People's Republic; the attitudes toward women there just aren't very good at all. Everyone thinks that just because it's a Communist country, socialist, whatever, that the women would be liberated. But they're not. Their whole attitude is that women are weaker than men, they're not as smart as men, they're just inferior. It's cultural, not political. It's been that way for thousands of years. I'd rather go out with American men any day.

ANTIGONE

(*off*)

Did Chen do something on the date that made you realize all this?

KIMI HU

No. I've known all this my whole life. My father is Chinese. He has a very superior attitude. He looks down his nose at anything female no matter what.

ANTIGONE

(*off*)

Did he try to kiss you?

KIMI HU

What? My father?

ANTIGONE

(*off*)

No! Chen. Did Chen try to kiss you?

KIMI HU

What do you mean "try"?

ANTIGONE

(*off*)

You know. Did you kiss?

KIMI HU

(*a little miffed*)

None of your damn business.

CUT TO

Chen in front of a black backdrop, sync-sound, speaking directly to Antigone.

ANTIGONE

(*off*)

So . . . Chen . . . how do you like American women?

CHEN

Good. Very nice. (*Smiles bashfully.*) Actually, I don't know very many American women. Some of them are very interesting.

ANTIGONE

(*off*)

Yeah. But do you *like* them? You know. Are you attracted to them?

CHEN

(*looking at camera*)

Could we . . . Billy? I must answer this? A little personal, I think.

BILLY
(*off*)

Yeah, okay.

ANTIGONE
(*off*)

Shit. What's the problem?

The camera stays on Chen, who looks blankly to one side, averting his eyes. Billy and Antigone have a soft conversation off: "Just start over." "You wanna cut?" "Nah. Keep rolling. Ask him something neutral. Ask him about football or something." At the word football, *Chen smiles.*

ANTIGONE
(*off*)

We understand you're interested in sports.

CHEN
(*still smiling*)

In America everyone is interested in sports, yes? In China we have sports too, of course, but not with such money, not pro sports, not television, like here. Every Sunday, two football games, every Saturday football, and other ones, bowling, golf, World Series we saw some of this year. But football I like best. Very unusual.

ANTIGONE

(*off*)

Have you been to a Browns game?

CHEN

No. Too expensive. Very expensive. Enough to eat for a week. . . . Much better I think to watch on TV.

CUT TO

A montage of TV images of football plays, sync-sound mixed very low, run over and over, forward and backward. A series of jump cuts of quarterbacks taking snaps, fading back to throw passes: Montana, Bradshaw, Theismann, Stabler.

CHEN

(*v.o.*)

. . . I like the Browns. Of course.

ANTIGONE

(*v.o.*)

The home team.

CHEN

(*v.o.*)

Yes. The hometown home team. . . . And I like the Redskins, because they are from D.C.

Joe Theismann takes a snap, rolls right.

ANTIGONE

(*v.o.*)

You're learning to play football yourself?

Theismann pumps twice, then lets fly a long pass.

CHEN

(*v.o.*)

Yes. Fun!

CUT TO

Chen running under a long pass in the front yard with Monty and Cortez on either side of him. He grabs and misses; the ball hits him in the chest and bounces off.

CHEN

(*v.o.*)

Mitchell teaches us how to play. We played today with the man downstairs, Mr. Little.

Series of quick shots of Chen and Tzu attempting to play touch football. They huddle with Mitchell; they run pass patterns; they fall down.

ANTIGONE

(*v.o.*)

Why didn't Mr. Wa play?

CHEN

(*v.o.*)

Wa does not like sports. Especially not American sports.

ANTIGONE

(*v.o.*)

You like sports, though?

CHEN

(*v.o.*)

You bet! Sports is good. But one thing . . .

CUT TO

Suzanne getting out of her blue 280-Z, waving, laughing. She catches an easy underhand pass, and then with only a bit of obvious effort, cocks her arm back and throws a perfect spiral to someone off-screen. Tzu applauds.

CHEN

(*v.o.*)

Why do they call it a *sports* car?

1

From Chen's window you can look out through a bare-branched elm to Donellan Avenue, a rutted, potholed thoroughfare for garbage trucks, metro buses, and snowplows on their way to refuel at the city garage two blocks down. After midnight, Chen, a ruefully resigned insomniac, would lie awake listening to the closing-time traffic, honks and whoops of drunks gunning it through the corner red light, the occasional backfire jerking him awake from uneasy dreams. Tzu and Wa had grown up in cities, so they were used to street noise, but Chen was a country boy, and his sleep suffered. (His occasional afternoon naps were tormented by the gritty hollow rumble of Monty Little's plastic Big Wheel tricycle on the sidewalk below—a booming hateful roar punctuated by high-pitched yelps and cries and voodoo chants.) Though he normally slept on his stomach like a child, he'd sometimes roll on his back to watch the full moon through his window, and who knows then what he might have thought, if not of his family and loved ones back in Heilongjiang Province, looking perhaps at the same moon? (I romanticize, of course: "the same moon" wouldn't be visible on the other side of the world; in northern China it would be midday, bright sunlight glancing off the snow; people would be closing their shops for lunch or practicing t'ai chi in the parks; his grandfather might be reading the paper, his mother chopping vegetables.) Chen's bed was a sturdy arrangement of plywood and concrete blocks, cross-braced with two-by-fours and topped with a junk-store twin-sized mattress *sans* box springs ("Not much bounce to it," Suzanne told me later in her matter-of-fact, thoughtless way); and he slept on this bounceless model of makeshift ingenuity under two blue blankets and a tattered gray quilt. On one side of the room stood a square bamboo laundry basket; next to it, on the floor, was a small mono tape player and a half-dozen neatly stacked borrowed cassettes (*Conversational English,* The Doobie Brothers, *Sgt. Pepper, The Bee Gee's Greatest Hits*—Chen discoing down in the shower, singing "Stayin' Alive" into his microphone fist). Over the basket, push-pinned in place, was his map of the city, with major bus routes highlighted in yellow marker and the red streets running everywhere and nowhere like raku cracks; above the bed hung a poster of three red poppies in a black vase, bought at the university bookstore's half-price sale. He sat often, I'm sure, in his motley Early American ladder-back chair (under its chipping outer coats of enamel you could discern patches of Day-Glo red, white, and blue, painted no doubt in a craze of counterculture patriotism by some now middle-aged flower-child). The chair stayed neatly tucked under a rickety pine desk when Chen wasn't working; when he was, he would stand and stretch every half-hour or so, and probably curse the stolid pil-grims who designed such upright seating. The rest was standard-issue contemporary American apart-ment, circa 1973: off-white walls and baseboards; wall-to-wall white shag carpet; a small closet with louvered doors. The only other object of note in Chen's room was his bookcase—a plain brown corrugated cardboard box resting on its side, fac-ing out toward the bed, with the book spines turned horizontally, stacked, not shelved. Four or five of them were Chinese, so I had no idea what they were (porn novels? math texts? the wit and wisdom of Mao Tse-tung?); but the others I'd heard about already, from Billy and Antigone: a fat red English-Chinese dictionary; a math text, *Advanced Calculus for Systems Applications*; a tat-tered paperback *Autobiography of Malcolm X*; my copy of *Huck Finn* with reproductions of the orig-inal edition illustrations; a small blue leather-bound *Hamlet*; Tzu's battered *Merriam-Webster International Dictionary of the English Language*; and Suzanne's *Leibniz: Monadology,* a lavender paperback. On top of the book-box lay a copy of a glossy football magazine, *Pigskin Weekly.* Beside that, with some blond soap star leering from the cover, a month-old *TV Guide.* And on the otherwise empty desk—not even a pencil, not even a paper clip—Chen's copy of the police report of his mugging, detailing his losses and injuries, and noting under ADDITIONAL REMARKS in the responding officer's labored scrawl, "Victim is Foreign Oriental."

I'd been there visiting his housemates. I excused myself, used their bathroom. Coming back down the hall I stopped and stood in Chen's open doorway, looking, until Tzu, concerned, came after me. I was memorizing Chen's room. I wanted to fix in my mind Suzanne's new milieu. I *wanted* that room—I couldn't help it—wanted every feature, every detail, wall to wall, floor to ceiling, chair to desk to books to bed.

Ever since Tzu told me, ever since I saw them walking brazenly hip to hip down our sidewalk (*my* sidewalk! in broad daylight!), I've been moping around the house, muttering a lot of rot and rehearsing a cynical laugh, wondering what the hell I'm doing in Cleveland. I'm not in love with Suzanne Betts and I keep telling myself to tell myself that—*You are not in love with her*—but seeing them together so unexpectedly caught me off guard, and I'm having trouble shrugging it off. I can't stop imagining them together, in her Jacuzzi of course, his dumpy, comical body wedged in one corner as she trembles above him, her damp hair rhythmically brushing his round astonished face; I envision them there, yes, despite myself, but elsewhere as well—strolling around the pond at the downtown park across from her office, holding hands at the movies, shopping together. I picture Chen driving her Z. I see him cooking her dinner and giving her foot massages. I imagine them slow dancing.

It's Friday night, two days after I find out, when she calls. I'm vegging out in front of some mindless made-for-TV movie, all drug deals and car chases, bimbos and hunks. "So, Dex," she says.

"So?" I say.

"So now you know."

"Let me turn down the TV, okay?" I don't wait for an answer. I set the phone down, reach for the remote and hit MUTE. A warehouse full of cocaine explodes in silent slow motion and the cops slap high-fives. I pick up the phone. "Okay," I say.

She asks how my Thanksgiving was. "Fine," I say. I ask about hers. "Fine." She sounds a little guilty, a little chagrined.

"Look, Dex," she says, "I'm just calling to make sure you're all right. Chen told me you were there the other day when I came by. So I guess you figured it out." She clears her throat. "I was going to tell you myself, but I've just been putting it off. You were out of town so long, and a lot can happen in two weeks."

"Apparently so," I say.

"Please don't be mad, okay? You sound really mad at me. You're not mad at me, are you?"

"I don't have any right to be mad at you, Suzanne."

"But you are anyway, aren't you?"

"I don't know," I say. "Mad? I guess. More like confused. I just can't figure you out."

"Me, either," she says earnestly. "Me, too. A lot of times I don't make sense to myself, even. It's been a really weird year, the weirdest year of my life, and it's made me a little crazy, I think. I'm nuts. I mean, really."

"You're not nuts, Suzanne. You just don't know what you want."

"Hmm. Well . . . maybe."

"Like when we first met, remember? You told me you didn't want to get involved with anyone and for me to back off, and then, practically overnight, you fall in love with Czapinczyk. And then you break up with him and come back into my life just long enough to get me interested, and—"

"Oh, Dex—"

"—now you're with Chen—"

She sighs. Neither of us speaks. Two cars careen silently around a city streetcorner, the second plowing through a sidewalk newsstand; magazines and newspapers go flying. I'm starting to feel really numb, and tell her so. "Oh, Dex, I'm sorry. I've hurt your feelings, haven't I?"

"Well," I say. "I'll get over it. It's okay."

"No, it's not okay. I'm really sorry. But you know I didn't do it on purpose."

I do know that. I never thought she did. But I swear that as she says this, a woman in the movie walks into a bar, orders a drink, then throws it in some guy's face. Cut to commercial: a Budweiser spot.

"Dex? You still there?"

"Yeah."

"You okay?"

"Yeah. Look, Suzanne, what have you told Chen about us?"

She hesitates. "Why?"

"I just want to know."

"Why?"

"Just so I know what to expect. How to act around him. Maybe I should go talk to him about things, just to clear the air, you know?"

"Please don't," she says. "I think it would really complicate things. I don't think he'd know quite how to handle it. He's pretty naïve in a lot of ways, Dex. He'd probably freak out."

"Oh." Something else explodes—a car, another warehouse?—and I zap the TV off. "Well. What do I do now? What do you want me to do?"

"That's easy," she says. "I want you to be my friend. I want you to be happy for me."

"Should I be? Are you happy?"

"Yes. I think so. I really think I am. Can't you tell? Maybe it's just temporary. Maybe we're too different. But he's really good for me. He needs me, and I've never had that before. . . . Look, I don't really feel right talking about this to you. I'm afraid I'm hurting your feelings."

"Suzanne," I say.

"What?"

"Are you in the bathtub?"

"What?"

"I can hear you splashing around in there."

She laughs, caught by surprise, a merry little mermaid.

"You *are* in the bathtub. On a Friday night."

"We were having a serious discussion," she says, and now I can definitely hear the slosh of water. "You know, I'm just trying to be fair here. So I don't think we should talk about him anymore. It's not really fair to you. Or to him, either. I don't talk to him about you."

I realize then how Chen can do this to his "good American friend." "He doesn't even know, does he? He has no idea we were lovers."

"No, he doesn't. All I've told him is that we're friends. And that's all he needs to know. Listen, Dex, you wanted an explanation. I'll try. You and I were going nowhere. That's why I started seeing Mick. And after we broke up, I tried it again with you but nothing really clicked, you know? It's not your fault, it's nothing you did or didn't do. You're a wonderful guy, you're sweet and cute and I really like you. But we're better off as friends. We just weren't going anywhere. That has nothing to do with Chen. I had no commitment to you. We only slept together twice."

Only! I don't know what to say.

"Christ, listen to me," she says. "I'm disgusted. I'm disgusted with myself. Maybe I shouldn't have called. Dex, can't you just let go? We weren't going anywhere anyway. Let go and wish me luck, just like I'll do for you. Please? You have a good heart. Be my friend. You're a good person, Dex. We're both bigger than this."

And so on, and so on, until we finally agree there's nothing left to say and we hang up. The kind of conversation that you memorize and re-play again and again to wring all the irony out of it, to kick yourself for sounding like bad TV dia-logue—my life as soap opera; life imitates dreck.

Medium shot: the camera slow-pans right, past a bookcase bare of books, past a rack of records and cassettes, to the twenty-two-inch TV in its oak veneer cabinet. "Media Center," Wa's voice-over says, "Me-di-a Center. Media."—and it is: a complete Home Entertainment System: the forty-plus-channel cable television wired for stereo sound, massive sound system with a megawatt power amp, turntable, reel-to-reel tape deck, cassette deck, phase-

linear graphic equalizer, wall-to-wall speakers, and, as the camera pans on a bit farther, a large-screen projection TV, a BetaMax and a VHS VCR—eight or ten thousand dollars worth of stuff, easy. The TV screen cycles through the channels without stopping, perhaps two seconds on each program, as Wa speaks voice-over.

WA

(*v.o.*)

Fifty, sisty channels. All from the chair, all remote. Up and down volume. A control that turns off the volume. A control that makes the picture bigger. Then to the right size again. Zoom, it is called zoom.

CUT TO

Close-up of Wa, against the black background, speaking directly to the camera. A note of disbelief throughout this speech.

WA

I am watching this. While my friend is watching TV I am watching him. And he stays at one channel, one program, only twenty, thirty seconds. He look at one thing. Say a baseball game. One time they throw the ball. The man tries to hit. He does not. He misses. My friend will change it. Next!

He makes a diagonal slice in the air, hand held as if for a karate chop.

Next channel is loud—static sound. Next! Next show—comedy. But why this is funny to him I don't understand because he watches only a minute. But he will laugh. He knows the characters, he knows the show, he knows these . . .

Groping for a word. He pushes at the bridge of his black horn-rims, then gives up, starts over.

The audience, they laugh and so he laugh and he change it. Or maybe some commercial. He talks to it. If a man might say that you should buy a car from me, my friend will talk back. He will say the man to *go to hell,* or maybe *eat me,* or he might say *bullshit* at the man. And change the channel.

Wa shakes his head.

And the same with music. And not just this friend, this one man. Everyone. Our neighbors, the other students, everyone, when they give us a ride I have seen them at the radio, change the channel of the song if you don't like it. And hit the button again and again.

He looks into the lights and his glasses glare over. He shakes his head again, waits.

ANTIGONE
(*off*)
So?

WA
(*with a tiny smile*)
So. That is the big problem of America.

Clearly he's been leading up to this. His eyes behind the glasses look triumphant.

The problem of America.

He looks straight at the camera again, snorts, and speaks suddenly in rapid Chinese, a shrill aspirated diatribe. After a few words, Wa's voice is mixed low under Billy's voice reading an English translation (provided by Kimi Hu and her bilingual dictionary). Wa's Chinese sentences are measured and forceful, with none of the awkwardness of his English.

TRANSLATOR

(v.o.)

The people of this country have no sense of continuity, no history. They move from moment to moment like butterflies among flowers, without memory or awareness; there is no sense of purpose, no discipline, only greed and self-indulgence. Their minds are cluttered and unfocused. This is from watching too much TV, among other things. TV has corrupted them, ruined their minds and misdirected their priorities. But I will not grieve for this culture. America is a barbaric nation, peopled by hedonists and sexual deviants, and the sooner it self-destructs, the better.

Wa has stopped speaking. He looks toward Antigone, off-camera, and takes a deep breath. He scrunches his mouth as if he's just bitten into a lemon. Abruptly he stands up.

ANTIGONE

(*off*)

What did you say? Would you please translate for us? Mr. Wa?

WA

Tank you.

He walks out of the shot. The camera remains focused on the black background. Off-camera, Billy yells, "Cut!"

3

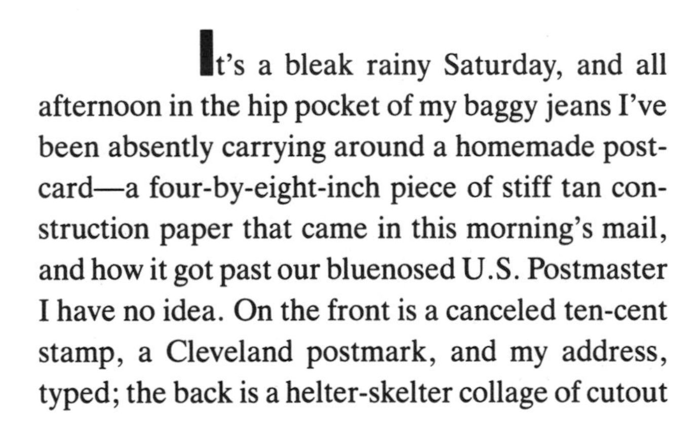

It's a bleak rainy Saturday, and all afternoon in the hip pocket of my baggy jeans I've been absently carrying around a homemade post-card—a four-by-eight-inch piece of stiff tan construction paper that came in this morning's mail, and how it got past our bluenosed U.S. Postmaster I have no idea. On the front is a canceled ten-cent stamp, a Cleveland postmark, and my address, typed; the back is a helter-skelter collage of cutout female body parts, mostly breasts and vulvas and buttocks clipped from skin mags, with an occasional hand or arm scattered here and there, and in one corner is a severed leg, bare foot arched forlornly. Slightly off-center, pasted to a full-body open-legged crotch shot, is a small photo of Suzanne's head, tilted at a grotesque angle. A violent red crayon scribble crisscrosses her face. Along the card's bottom edge I read the typed words SAT DEC 6. Three guesses who sent it, and the first two don't count.

I slept badly last night. In the first gray hour of day I finally drifted off and dreamed myself into Suzanne's wondrous bathtub, where she and I sat and talked without touching and forgave each other our thoughtless offenses, our insensitivities. Chen was there too, as a small strange creature with tiny webbed finlike hands, and he swirled and frolicked in and out of the bubbles like some happy porpoise. Like a porpoise, I said to Suzanne, pointing, and the instant I said it, with perfect dream logic he came up for air in Suzanne's arms and she kissed him sweetly on his forehead, by his blowhole. Off to the side, Czapinczyk filmed the whole thing with Billy's camera. . . . This freakish dream had haunted me all morning, so when Zap's sick postcard came, I somehow wasn't surprised. It was all a bad joke, so I laughed, Ha ha, and creased the card twice and shoved it in my pocket; I've been sitting on it ever since.

When six o'clock rolls around, I head next door, ostensibly to borrow a cup of rice for my solo Saturday bachelor dinner, but with half a mind toward seeing Chen, getting things out in the open and wishing him well. But he's out for the evening, and Tzu, no fool, puts down his Rubik's Cube (these things are everywhere!) and looks at me sadly; I can't help asking, "Suzanne?"

Before he can answer there's a shout from the downstairs hallway, followed by a howl of childish laughter and a door slam that shakes the whole building. In a few clamorous seconds Wa stomps his way up the stairs, crashes into the living room, and flings his briefcase furiously at the plaid sofa. He begins hissing at Tzu in Chinese, then switches to English when he sees me: "Mitchell, you know the boy Monty. Downstairs, the black boy. Whenever he sees me he will . . . he . . ."

"Make motions," Tzu supplies.

"His eyes are terrible," Wa says. He drops into an armchair, shaking his head angrily.

"We thought at first he was playing," Tzu says. "But now he seems serious. He sings, too. It is not in English, I think. But he sings at Wa."

"Voodoo," I say, and they each repeat "Voodoo?" and wait for my explanation, but all I can summon up are dumb movie images of human sacrifice and frenzied dancing, mojos and gris-gris and wild-looking black women in trances. "Yeah, voodoo," I say, and spell it for them. "It's not really a religion, exactly, but it has a lot of semireligious elements to it. I guess it's kind of like black magic—I mean, black like evil, not black like Negro . . . although, come to think of it, it is a black-people kind of thing, too. . . . I'm not making any sense, am I?"

"Maybe," Tzu says uncertainly.

"It is dangerous?" Wa asks.

"Well, no, I don't think so. I wouldn't worry too much about it. He's just a kid having some fun."

"Not such fun for me!" Wa says.

"It'll be okay." I imagine Monty sticking pins through a little Wa doll, complete with slanty eyes and black glasses. "Just don't let him get any of your hair."

"Hair?" Wa, stricken, delicately pats at his crew cut.

"God, yes. If he gets hold of your hair, you're a goner."

"Goner?" Tzu asks, and then reads through my best poker face: "Mitchell, you are joking with us."

Well, yeah. I promise them I'll speak to Monty.

"Today?"

"Soon. Don't worry."

"Okay. Thank you, Mitchell," Wa says, sincerely grateful, and I feel a twinge of guilt about putting him on. He lets out a long sigh, smiles brightly, heads for the kitchen to start water for tea.

"We were speaking of Chen," Tzu calls after him. "And Suzanne."

Wa reappears holding a tin teapot. He shakes his head, sucks in his cheeks—a disapproving old man.

"It's really none of my business," I offer, idly twisting Tzu's Rubik's Cube.

Tzu shrugs. (Is this a Chinese motion, I wonder? Sometimes his gestures seem tinged with a Slavic melancholy, testament to his four lonely years studying in Russia . . . or did he pick up this sad half-shrug from some American sitcom, a TV bit?)

"We make a mistake with Chen," Wa tells me. "He is not married."

Wa and Tzu are. In fact, they're both proud Pops, one kid each—and cute little tykes they are, too, one clutching a bamboo fishing pole, the other flying a red kite in the coffee-table photo cube. Devoted fathers, Wa and Tzu call home once a month (all they can afford), and mope for days afterward. They miss their wives. They could no more fall in love with Western women than could Chairman Mao. "Their makeup makes me sneeze," Tzu told me once, and Wa tactlessly agreed: "They're ugly."

Compared to them, Chen's a kid, like me—twenty-four, single, no family beyond Mom and Grandpa—and he's impressionable. "Confused," Wa says. "He confuses him."

"She," Tzu says.

"Yes. *She* confuses him."

"Bad situation," Tzu says. "Wa and I were trusted to take care of him."

"It'll blow over," I predict. "It's just a phase."

"Just a face?" Wa asks.

"His face," Tzu explains. "That Suzanne wants."

"No," I say, "just a *phase.* A cycle."

"Oh." Tzu says one word of Chinese.

"Oh," Wa says. "It is bad Chen have come here. America."

Yes.

4

In Tzu's bedroom, furnished much like Chen's yet even more Spartan, we look up the word *voodoo* in Venerable Webster's. A few lines about this dictionary, the mainstay of my neighbors' linguistic knowledge: between its two tattered covers are nestled not only the definitions and etymologies of over 100,000 English words, but also an encyclopedia of biographical names; a rhyming dictionary; a directory of U.S. and Canadian universities; a brief grammar handbook; a metric conversion chart; a "Pronouncing Gazetteer Containing More Than Ten Thousand Names of Places," with 1960 census population figures; a list of forms of address for dignitaries, public officials, and religious figures (the proper address for a divorced woman: "ordinarily Mrs. with her maiden name as a prename instead of her husband's prename"); and even an "Etymology of Common English Given Names," wherein Dexter is listed as Latin for "on the right hand, fortunate" and Suzanne derives from the Hebrew for "graceful lily." This most excellent stockpile of lexicographical and cultural odds and ends has seen better days—the binding is broken, the first few pages are ripped, and the once navy blue cover has faded to white like an old pair of jeans—but Tzu never tires of leafing through at random, committing to his phenomenal memory various English esoterica and underscoring each word as he reads with the long yellow nail of his pinky; and now when he finds *voodoo* (between *vomit* and *vora-*

cious, across the page from a spectral line drawing of a *vulture*), he lets out a pleased sigh, reads the definition silently, smiles at me, and then carefully intones: "Voodoo. One: a religion derived from African ancestor worship, practiced chiefly by Negroes of Haiti, and characterized by propitiatory rites and communication by trance with animalistic deities. Two: the practice of witchcraft." Then we had to look up *propitiatory,* which I had confused with *proprietary,* and then Tzu insisted on flipping through the pronouncing gazetteer until he came to *Haiti,* wedged between *Haiphong, Vietnam,* and *Hakodate, Japan.* "Little does not come from Haiti?" he asks me.

"Not as far as I know."

"Is it serious, this voodoo?"

I shrug. "Only if you believe in it."

"Ah. Like God. Do you believe, Mitchell? In God?"

"I believe it doesn't matter if I believe."

"You believe . . . ha. I see. But does it matter that you believe this?"

I look at him a little warily. All I really wanted was a cup of rice. "I thought religion was the opiate of the people," I say.

"Actually there are many opiates," Tzu says, smiling. "Could it be that the Theory of Possible Worlds is one?"

5

Chen had explained the whole concept at dinner one night a few weeks ago. Wa of course dismissed it immediately ("A trick of the white devils!" I imagine him snarling), but Tzu saw what an impression Possible Worlds had made on Chen, so he listened, probed, and questioned, and kept an open mind. When he asked Suzanne about it the next time she dropped by, she quoted Leibniz and suggested he read her copy of the

Monadology, over which Chen had been laboring even then. "Of course already I knew of him," Tzu tells me now, and seeing my politely raised eyebrows he recites, "Gottfried Wilhelm von Leibniz, German philosopher, 1646 to 1716. He invented the first computer. A kind of mechanical calculating machine. And also created calculus." I thought Isaac Newton— "No. Leibniz. And also he completed the first Chinese–German dictionary. Humorous, some of his errors in definitions. For example, he translates the word *zhong,* well-known name of a kind of fish—" and here Tzu explains in interminable detail the exact nature of the error, how it occurred and what makes it comic in Chinese, but something gets lost in the English translation. I smile, shake my head to show amusement: that Leibniz! what a card!

"Of course, this dictionary is minor compared to his other work. He did important mathematic theory, still used today. And symbolic logic, now necessary for computer programming. There is much to learn from Leibniz."

"So it seems," I say.

Tzu carefully replaces Venerable Webster's between two brick bookends and leans back against the edge of his desk. "You know, there are many Christians in China. Millions, perhaps. Unofficial, of course, but the concept of your God—pardon! the *Christian* god—it is known to many. I myself at one time . . ." He smiles at me, then sighs. "But this God taught by the Western missionaries has blue eyes and white skin. Also, as I am a scientist, I am taught not to believe. Especially if I ever want to become a Party member. So."

"Perhaps," I say slowly, "in another possible world, you could be both a Christian and a Party member."

"Clearly." Now he grins broadly. "There is, after all, a possible world for every combination, every situation. In another possible world, *you* could be a Party member. Or anything. There are infinite worlds. But Mitchell, Leibniz says this world is the *best* of all possible worlds. It is a logical argument if the existence of God is a given. Perfect logic, yes? 'God is perfect. God cannot do anything that is not perfect. God created this world. Therefore this world is perfect. Therefore this is the best of all possible worlds.' "

I've heard all this before from Suzanne. It seems absurd to me now, pointless, like arguing how many angels can dance on the head of a pin. I tell Tzu anybody who thinks this world is perfect has got a screw loose.

"Yes. To us it is not perfect, this world. Death and hunger and sorrow. War, hate. But we cannot know what is perfect to God, and what is not." The fact is, Tzu explains, that God, being all-knowing, can contemplate an infinite number of possible worlds, and he chose to create this one over others because it was the best. We can't say that a world without evil would be better than this world; in fact, without the evil we would be unable to value or appreciate the good. Every evil has its purpose. We cannot know what other kinds of worlds might be possible because only God knows what is and is not best, and therefore the whole problem comes down to—

"Faith," I say.

Tzu touches his fingertips together, nods. "Yes."

"Like everything else in religion. You have to trust God."

"Yes. To trust that God knew this world was perfect." He stands. "But for me, the argument begins on the false premise that God exists. I cannot understand why Chen does not see this. In the logical view—"

Suddenly for no reason I see Suzanne, bare-breasted at my mirror a month ago, smoothing a smear of pale lip gloss with the tip of her little finger.

6

It is indeed a sorry state of affairs when, despite your youth and flush pockets and relative good looks, you have resigned yourself for one reason or another to a tedious Saturday night alone on the sofa, and you find after listlessly flipping channels for an hour or so that television, your old reliable standby (and former medium of employment), has let you down. It *is* a wasteland sometimes. I'm hoping for a good *Saturday Night Live,* but as Belushi and Ackroyd rip through the first skit, I idly think of everyone else in America who's watching, and that leads me to Suzanne and Chen, who are almost certainly watching as well, unless they're *not* watching, otherwise engaged in the flickering TV light. This line of thought depresses me, so I'm actually glad when Czapinczyk calls. Before he can get started, I tell him to stop bothering me, that I haven't been out with Suzanne in weeks, that Chen Li-zhong is the new heir apparent to these midnight phone threats and high school acts of vandalism. At first he won't believe me, asks me how I liked his postcard, says he'll play me a tape of him and Suzanne in bed: Listen. I hang up. I've drifted to sleep on the sofa when he calls back to say with his warped logic that Suzanne has her phone off the hook, so it must be true about her and Chen.

"I can't believe it," he keeps muttering. "A goddamn Chink. I'm seriously thinking about calling the cops, having him deported."

I'm drowsy, hardly listening.

"There's laws against this sort of thing. Fornication, sodomy. Miscegenation."

"Illegal aliens," I mumble.

"Wait a minute," Czapinczyk says. "Wait. This is Chen, right? The one I met at the Halloween party? The one who got mugged?"

"Why?" I'm suddenly awake, wary.

"Yeah. That's him. I got him now. The one who got mugged, the Commie junior scientist. He's a fucking spy, is what he is. Him and his roommates both."

"How do you figure that?"

"Well, look. What are these Chinese over here to study?"

"SSM. Systems Science."

"Technology."

"Okay," I say. "So?"

"You ever ask what technology?"

"Sure. Hydroelectric. Radar. Like in airports."

"Right. Radar, right. Know what else? Cybernetics. Feedback loops."

"Speak English."

"Guidance systems. For missiles. They're milking our technology."

"Come on." I'm staring at the fuzzy snow of my after-hours TV. "They study thermostats, air-conditioning, stuff like that."

"The principles are the same. A circuit's a circuit. Any technology has military applications. Look, it's a perfect setup. Instead of spies, you send students. Instead of undercover, they're aboveboard. Instead of breaking the code they just learn the language and sit in the classroom."

"Okay." I yawn.

"You think this is funny, don't you, Mitchell? You like the idea of him fucking her?"

"Look, Zap—"

"That's Czapinczyk to you, buddy."

"Look, *Zap.*" I wait but all I hear is his steady breath. "I'm hanging up now."

"Yeah, you like it. You enjoy knowing he's in bed with her. Gives you something to think about. You're sick, man. You're a sick man, man. Well, I'm so glad we could have this little chat together. I guess I won't be needing to call *you* anymore."

"Right," I say, "not me," and then, in a pique of irony I'll regret later, I start Czapinczyk on his inexorable path toward Chen. I tell him my neighbors' phone number.

7

At three-thirty on the penultimate Sunday afternoon of his life, an unseasonably warm, bright day, Chen comes over to borrow my cousin's plumber's helper, which he asks for as "the thing to fix the water when it is broken," pantomiming with an up-and-down motion. I have to rummage—under the sink, in the hall closet—but finally track it down on the back fire-escape landing. It's the first time I've seen him since I found out, and for some reason I feel complete detachment—no anger, no jealousy, no animosity, no warmth. Nothing. I'm polite, that's all.

I notice his black eye has faded. "Yes," he says.

We don't seem to have much to say to each other. I decide Suzanne has told him that we'd dated and he feels awkward about it, so as he's heading for the door I ask if anything's wrong.

"No," he says, but then he wonders aloud whether I'd watched the news this morning. I hadn't. "Today is the thirty-ninth anniversary of the Pearl Harbor. Japan, the . . . sneak attack?"

"Yes," I say. "So?"

"So Wa says we should not go outside. Because Americans cannot see the difference of Chinese and Japanese. And . . . you know." He touches his eye gingerly.

"That's paranoia," I say, even though I remember some street wino calling Wa a dirty little Jap. "You tell Wa that's paranoia. Nobody even remembers Pearl Harbor. Anybody still mad about Pearl Harbor is too old and feeble to give you any trouble."

"Okay," Chen says, still rubbing his eye.

"So don't worry about it."

"Okay." He thanks me and turns to go. I can't help it: I ask him how Suzanne is doing.

He blinks three times at me, rapidly, confused, and I see I'm wrong: she hasn't told him. "You know," I say. "Suzanne."

Chen coughs. "Suzanne?"

"Yeah. Suzanne. That you went shopping with."

"Oh. Yes. He is fine."

"When did you last see him?"

"He is coming here this afternoon."

"Tell him hi for me," I say.

When he returns the plunger a half-hour later, his mood has improved; he seems his usual cheerful self. Tzu is with him and they're chattering in Chinese. "Do you know how to play," Chen asks me, "spring semester in-ter-murl football?"

"Why?"

"There is an SSM inter-murl team? And they want us to play."

"We thought maybe you could teach us," Tzu says hopefully.

"Me?"

"Why not?"

I can't think of a thing to say. Finally I hear myself telling Tzu that I can't imagine him playing football. "It would be good for the department," he tells me.

"When's the first game?"

"In January? Are you too busy, maybe?"

"No, no—"

"We only thought, because we knew you—"

"—and that you would teach us better—"

Of course: they'd rather embarrass themselves in front of me. They're afraid their Systems Science and Math buddies would laugh them off the practice field. So they come to me, knowing I can be trusted to do them right. I guess I should be flattered.

"Please, Mitchell?"

I shrug. "Okay," I say.

They grin with glee and I feel a flash of disgust. Oh, they're like kids, my Red Chinese;

they're so gullible sometimes, and the smallest things bring them pleasure.

"Now?" Chen asks. "This afternoon?"

"What about Suzanne," I say, just to devil him. "Don't you have plans?"

"After," he says. "Later."

"Oh." I give up. Get over it, I tell myself. "You got any tennis shoes?"

Chen smiles wider. "Adidas."

Adidas!

"And I have cloth shoes," Tzu offers.

"Good. Go put them on. And some old clothes. Tell Wa, make sure he's dressed right. You got a ball?"

"You do not have one?" Tzu asks.

They probably think everybody in America has one. They were astonished last month to find that I didn't own a Frisbee.

"I know—it's okay. I'll borrow one."

"Borrow?" Chen asks.

"From Little. The guy downstairs. The black man."

8

But downstairs the reggae is so loud that I don't bother beating on Little's door—he'd never hear me. The ball is lying in Monty's hallway junk pile, a treacherous and ever-changing heap of plastic cars and planes, strips of H.O. railroad track, a broken set of shoulder pads, and (today, anyway) a pair of wet moon boots and a Darth Vader helmet. Eventually (soon) someone descending the stairs (me) is going to break something (my neck), tripping on one of these items (a Wiffle-ball bat or GoBots from hell). I liberate the football and remind myself to speak to Monty about his voodoo war with Wa and to Little about lawsuits and liability insurance.

As I'm waiting for the Chinese, Billy and Antigone pull up and start unloading their movie gear. I ask if they're filming today. "Don't know," Billy says. Another scene in the film is the last thing I want right now, but when I tell him we're playing football, Billy perks up. "We need some more footage. Wa walked off the set that day and won't come back, and Chen has been avoiding me ever since he got mugged. If I can just film you guys playing, I won't have to do any interviews."

"I'm not much in the mood for it," I say, but he just grins and starts setting up the Arriflex.

"Hi, Antigone," I say. She's wearing maroon sweatpants and a tight black tank top under her unbuttoned jean jacket; I'm in love with her collarbones.

"Hey, Dex. How you doing?"

"I'm okay."

"No you're not," she says. "I see you making those bad eyes at me. What's wrong?"

"Nothing," I say, but then she looks so hurt that I tell her. "I just found out Suzanne is sleeping with Chen."

"Ha!" Antigone yelps. "I *told* you, Billy."

"Suzanne Betts?" Billy asks.

"Just like I told you."

"Christ," I say. "Did everybody know it but me? How did *you* find out?"

"I just knew," Antigone says, giving me a consolation kiss on the cheek.

"She's psychic," Billy tells me.

Chen and Tzu come tramping down the stairs. They look unhappily at the camera, Chen especially, but they shake Billy's hand politely and make little half-bow nods to Antigone, who throws them back a mock little half-curtsy. (Tzu, later: "Is the American custom to shake a woman's hand? Or embrace? Or only greet verbally?" Beats the hell outa me.) We all smile a bit too brightly at each other. "Where's Wa?" I ask.

"Not interested," Chen blurts. Tzu shrugs: "He does not want to play."

"It's too American for him, isn't it?"

"Wa has contempt for games with balls," Tzu explains.

It's too American for him.

I kick absently at a clump of brown grass, wondering what I've gotten myself into. How do you explain football? It's more intricate than chess, abstract as a computer program. Anything can happen. Tzu and Chen are not stupid. They're crack students in a highly technical field. Their English is good. They catch on quick. But football! Where do you start?

Well, I pick up the ball. "This is how you hold it," I say, and they nod. "These are called laces."

Wa saunters outside to watch disdainfully. He will not play, though his roommates ask him several times.

"Okay, forget it," I say. "Let's just throw a few."

We spread out and I toss Tzu a pass. Of

course he drops it. He cocks the ball back, stiff-armed, aims it toward Chen; the ball falls to the ground. Antigone laughs. It's hopeless. They'll be eaten alive. The SSM team just wants them to fill up space—as stopgaps, grunts. At best they'll warm the bench. At worst they'll play the line and be battered and bashed by big frat-rat jocks, tough, red-meat-eating Americans who've spent their long adolescences sacking quarterbacks and blocking kicks.

But if I can teach them to run pass patterns maybe their team will use them for decoys. Maybe they'll be able to duck the dangerous skirmishes in the line of scrimmage and get downfield where it's less cluttered, safer. So with Billy's camera rolling and Antigone aiming the shotgun mike, I show them what I know—buttonhooks, turnouts, easy stuff. Every now and then they're able to catch one. "The ball is a bad shape," Tzu says apologetically.

"What do you guys play in China?" I ask. "Ping-Pong, right?"

"Pardon?"

"Table tennis?"

"Yes," Chen answers. "And volleyball. Everyone plays."

"Except Wa. Right, Wa?" I call. Wa has contempt for games with balls.

Billy is reloading when Cortez Little appears in his daddy's doorway. He's dressed in black, top to toe—ski mask, nylon jacket, sweatpants, black sneakers—and Chen jumps at his shrill indignant voice. "Hey!" Cortez yells. "Hey!"

We all look at him.

"Hey, that ain't yours!"

"What ain't?" I say.

"That football. That's mine."

"Oh, yeah?"

"Yeah."

"Huh," I say.

"Lemme see that ball."

I squat, one hand on the ball, look him in the eye. Monty suddenly appears from nowhere, leans against the porch railing, and puts his thumb in his mouth. "Lemme see that ball!" Cortez yells.

"It's not yours," I say, and hold it up to show

the name written in squiggly black Magic Marker: mOntEZUmA l.

"Tha's a lie," Cortez says. "I'monna tell my dad you stole my ball."

"Go ahead."

He strides to their front door and pushes against it with his hip. It's locked. We all watch him beat furiously against it with both fists. Wa smirks. "Y'all in trouble now," Monty says, ritually curling his fingers and lifting one leg like a pissing dog.

Chen looks at me nervously. "Maybe we should give the ball."

"I told you not to play," Wa hisses.

The door opens and Cortez's father stands there yelling: "Boy, I told you to go out and play and stop disturbing me!" "But Dad, they got our ball." "You're about to make me very angry here, Cortez. . . ." Then he notices us, looking from face to face until he catches my eye. Little steps out into the yard. He stops. He says, "All three of you Chinese fellows are out here, eh? There's no one in your apartment, and you left your damned TV on, going full blast. Don't you know there's an energy crisis in this country? You all ought to be lined up against a wall and shot."

Nobody says a word. Nothing. I can't decide whether Little's serious or not. Someone—Billy? Tzu?—coughs twice. I walk over to Little and hand him the ball. He stares at me hard for a second, steps up so close he can breathe in my face, and then breaks into a grin, sheepish, shy—and I can't help grinning back at him and he says, "How about a game, sport?"

And we're both grinning like idiots.

"My boys and I will stand all of you. Two-hand touch below the belt. No razzle-dazzle, one run per series, three completes a first. One-man rush unless the passer fumbles; rusher counts four Mississippis. Play to three touchdowns or until it gets dark."

"An' no feel golds," Cortez says.

"You guys want to play?" I ask the Chinese.

"Yes," Tzu says excitedly. "Chen too."

Chen glances from Little to me to Little again. He says a word or two, softly, to Tzu, who stares at him in apparent wonder.

"Okay," Chen says tentatively.

"Your funeral," I say, turning back to Little. "How about two-hand touch anywhere? And just two completes for a first down, 'cause these guys have never played before."

"You're breaking my heart, Mitchell."

"Hey, come on, man. Look at 'em, they'd never even touched a football 'til half an hour ago."

He inclines his head and looks at me knowingly over the rims of his gold glasses. "All right, sport. Whatever you like."

"And no Mississippis. Too hard for them to say."

"Tough titty," Monty says. His brother kicks him.

"We can say it," Tzu tells me.

"You understand this?" I ask. "Before you can rush the passer, you have to count, like this:

One-Mississippi, two-Mississippi, three-Mississippi, four-Mississippi. You count as fast as you can and then you try to tag the guy with the ball, but you can't rush him until you finish counting."

"Not a problem," Tzu says.

"You sure?"

"Sure."

We set the boundaries and toss a coin. "It's heads, gentlemen," Little says. "We kick off to you. Let's go, boys."

Lining them up hurriedly, I try to explain the kickoff to Tzu and Chen. Little points at Wa, who's still leaning against the building, sulking. "What about him?"

"Play with us, Wa," Tzu calls, but Wa shakes his head slowly.

"Please, Wa," Chen adds.

"*Bu*!" he says emphatically.

"Go on, kick it," I yell. Cortez drops his arm, Little's leg snaps up, and with a hollow *thud!* the ball explodes into the gray sky, lofting higher and higher, Cortez and Monty under it running fiercely toward us with Antigone cheering them on and Billy swinging his camera wildly, and only in that instant do I belatedly realize—fool!—that the game will be a disaster.

9

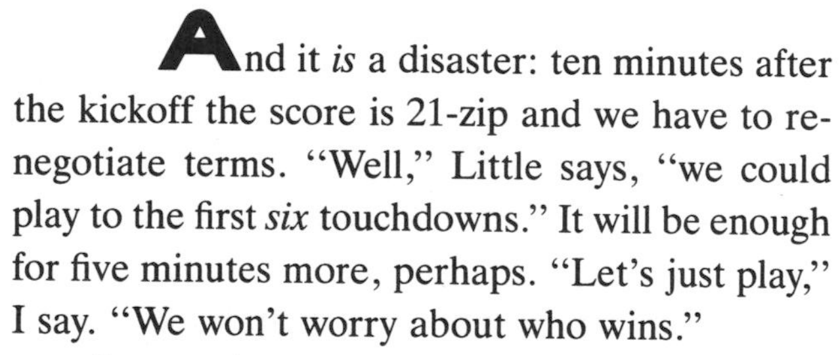

And it *is* a disaster: ten minutes after the kickoff the score is 21-zip and we have to renegotiate terms. "Well," Little says, "we could play to the first *six* touchdowns." It will be enough for five minutes more, perhaps. "Let's just play," I say. "We won't worry about who wins."

So we play. And soon only Monty can remember the score: vindictive brat, every few minutes he taunts us with, "We *slaughtering* y'all now."

I send Tzu up to rush although he can barely count his Mississippis. "Just watch the ball. Don't let him around you." Slyly, Little sends his sons on a crisscross; Chen and I bump in midfield; Cortez gets behind me, snags the pass, and picks up twenty yards before I can run him out-of-bounds.

On the next play I hang back, giving Monty a lot of running room, and when the pass comes in, lobbed low and easy, I dig in, cut hard, and, falling forward, reach in front of him to scoop the ball into my arms.

"Trap!" Monty yells. "You trapped it!"

"No he didn't," his father says. "That was one of the prettiest pickoffs you'll ever see, too."

It's their first turnover.

"What happened?" Tzu asks, worried. "Ours again?"

I send them downfield and put the ball in the air.

Little rushes, counting Mississippis with his precise enunciation. I scramble. Finally Chen breaks clear. Cortez is coming up fast, so I have to drill it, but it's a perfect pass: I hit him right in the chest. Chen drops it. "*Catch* the goddamn ball," I yell. "It hurt," he says.

We huddle up; I kneel and they watch me draw diagrams in the dirt. "Tzu, you center, then go out about five steps and just turn around. And Chen, you run a zigzag. Like this. Head straight for the tree."

He does. I burn it past Little's outstretched arms into the roots of our front-yard elm and Chen dives for it. He comes up scraped, muddy, and empty-handed. "Same play," I tell him in the huddle. "Right into the tree. Catch it this time." He doesn't. Watching for the pass he nearly dislocates his shoulder on the tree trunk; the ball skitters into the street past Cortez, who smiles and nods at Chen and points to it: Fetch, boy. Chen fetches, slowly. "Shame on you, Mitchell," Antigone yells from the sidelines, shaking her head so her dreadlocks dance. "Shame!"

"What?"

"I see what you're doing."

"What?" I say.

"I see what you're doing. And I see why, too. And you should be ashamed."

Little looks at her, then at me, then at her again, then laughs. "Fourth down," he announces.

"Let's do the flea-flicker," Tzu says.

"Not enough player," Chen mutters, brushing bark from his hair.

Tzu points at Wa. I shake my head.

"Maybe Suzanne will play," Chen says, "when she gets here," and as he speaks her blue 280-Z magically pulls up to the curb and she pops out, wearing boots and purple tights and a long camel-hair coat, and dangly silver earrings that play hide-and-seek in her hair. Billy zooms in on her and she tells him with a leisurely gesture to kiss off. Little whistles. "Spunky," he says, then on the next play sacks me, big-time, before I can even set up.

"Looks like the Communists need a little expertise," Suzanne says, smiling. I don't answer.

"Soon we will catch a pass," Chen tells her hopefully.

"Now they have it again?" Tzu asks.

"Yeah. You cover Cortez. I got Monty. Chen, you rush. Get up there, hurry. Count your Mississip—"

"Hut! Hut!"

"*Count,* Chen!"

"One Mississississi—"

"Cortez!"

"Two Mississ—"

"Go, Cortez, go!"

"—ree Missi—"

"TD! Aw*right,* Cortez! We *slaughtering* y'all now."

"Four Mississississi."

Wa laughs.

10

But finally we complete a pass, a quick turnout to Chen: I toss it soft; the ball hangs, fat, brown as bread; Chen reaches out; it bounces off his down vest into his hands; he bobbles it excitedly, drops to one knee, and suddenly he has it. Monty tags him. And then, as if on signal, the game breaks up: laughing, Little allows that they've had enough. Chen surprises Suzanne with a big kiss, like the quarterback kissing the head cheerleader; Wa and Tzu look away, embarrassed. "Nice catch, Chen," I say, but the irony is lost on everyone but me.

"Your guys didn't do half bad," Little tells me.

Yeah, I think. They didn't.

Everyone troops back inside. I stand for a moment on the dusky lawn, then bring up the rear behind Chen and his girl. It's slow going, due to all of Billy's equipment. Halfway up the stairs Suzanne looks back over her shoulder to throw me a sad, apologetic little smile. Chen doesn't notice. He's preoccupied, surreptitiously stroking her hip under cover of the camel-hair coat.

"See you later," I tell them at the landing. And I turn back alone to my cousin's clean, elegant apartment, where all the lights are burning. Where the heat's on full force, the refrigerator's full of food, the radio plays all the hits. Where there is no energy crisis. Where through the thin walls I can hear their TV blaring out the heartbeat, the pulse, of our homeland, Chen's and mine—America.

Medium shot: Tzu folding his laundry at the kitchen table, setting it aside in neat stacks. Over his shoulder at the edge of the frame we can see the tiny black-and-white TV flickering in the living room. No sync-sound.

TZU

(*v.o.*)

I have learned much about the true America since we came here. In China, we have certain ideas about Americans and American life, about, say, capitalism and racial injustice, and so on. Sex and violence. I am afraid that some of these . . . ideas . . . are true. So. But this culture, it is complex, infinitely complex, many subsystems interacting. Immense, yet subtle. To speak in general about it is far too simplistic.

In the living room, Chen flops down in front of the TV. Tzu finishes his laundry, hoists his basket, and walks out of the shot.

TZU

(*v.o.*)

Within a system, everything has meaning. There are random variables, yes, but random is still meaningful. Our difficulty is to interpret, to understand. What is the word? In French you would say *obsession*?

ANTIGONE

(v.o.)

Obsession? Obsessed?

TZU

(v.o.)

Yes. Americans are obsessed with sex.

CUT TO

Close-up of color television images, from commercials, movies, sitcoms, soaps: actresses in lingerie pitching toiletries, a muscled male torso soaping itself in the shower, frantic couples rolling around under twisted sheets, women getting dressed. The shots jump quickly, no more than two seconds each, like the football montage earlier. Tzu's voice-over continues.

TZU

(*v.o.*)

And violence. You know Mr. Chen was beaten and robbed?

Now the sexual images are crosscut with violent images: a black boxer smashes a white boxer in slow motion; a redheaded woman lifts one long leg from a bubble bath; a swarthy gangster turns the key of a car, which explodes; a white woman in boxer shorts rolls on top of a white man and kisses him with her mouth open; an Arab fanatic sprays a crowd of kids with an Uzi and gets blown away in turn by a white cop.

TZU

(*v.o.*)

Why? Americans have too many guns. Too easy to get one. (*Sarcastically.*) But everyone has a gun, so we need one too. For protection. Much of the violence here I believe is because of injustice and class struggle. In China many people believe that violence and sex are the result of bad economics, capitalism, and that they are the signs of decadence. We have very little violence there, not since the Cultural Revolution.

CUT TO

Medium shot of their closed apartment door. We can just make out their names on the hand-lettered sign.

ANTIGONE

(*v.o.*)

But there must be some kinds of violence in China.

TZU

(*v.o.*)

Mr. Chen is now afraid to go outside.

1

Tuesday after our football game I bump into Tzu on the street: as it happens, we're both post office–bound—I to pick up a package, he to buy stamps. We shake hands, ask after each other's health. He tells me their bathroom sink is still clogged and wonders if I'd be so kind . . . "Plumbing to me is a mystery," Tzu says. "Electrical, yes, heating and cooling, okay, but water . . ." I remember my father teaching me the three rules of plumbing—"hot left, cold right, shit flows down"—and wonder what Tzu would make of that. "I'll drop by later," I say, "with some Drāno and a monkey wrench."

It's early on a bright, blustery morning. Traffic lights swing and bounce on their black cables. Wind lifts women's skirts and blows sheets of newsprint like tumbleweeds against our legs. Walking in wind like this always makes me happy, but Tzu looks pensive. "It is very dirty today," he says. "So much trash." Gum foil glints in the litter like coins. Candy labels and tattered magazine pages skitter away. A green-eyed woman's face with a footprint on it. Discarded cellophane wrappers like shed skin, colored plastic smashed like eggshells. We crunch through bottle shards, glinting teardrops of drink-can pop-tops, flattened boxes, all the slough of packaging. Tzu nearly treads in dog shit. I kick a stove-in milk carton. Beer cans roll over drunkenly on their dents, caroming off each other, blowing in semicircles. At the curb a wave of trash is piled like floodwater against a dam, momentarily stalled in its eastward drift. I'd never noticed. "Is there so much litter in China?"

"No. Men who clean come daily. They sweep the streets. And everyone saves the trash, for what is valuable. Not like here."

"Wa would say we have more trash because of our materialist culture."

Tzu makes his Slavic shrug. "Wa is a thinker. A poet. Also a very good scientist and he understands much more about the United States than either I or Chen. Wa sees the evil in your country and it makes him stronger, but he will not see any good here. Chen is the opposite. He does not know very well yet what he is doing."

"And you?"

"Ah ha ha ha."

Yes, I know, Tzu: you're the middleman. For you there is no cut-and-dried, no black-and-white. Good and evil are always qualified. Things are complicated. Though you're a full-fledged Marxist-Leninist-Maoist proletariat hero, you're above cant; you can kick through the profligate American trash on the way to the post office with a running dog of imperialism and still call him friend. "I can suspend my ideologies," he says. "China is my home and so I like it better than America. But I like America too. You and I, we are both men together and not enemies."

I touch his shoulder, smile, nod. Then an old gritty bum steps out in front of us, raises his grimy arms out to each side, cries, "Sirs! Mr. Whitemans. Can you gimme a dollar?"

Tzu stops. "Keep walking," I tell him out of the side of my mouth.

"A dollar. Just a dollar. I know you got it."

"Sorry," I say.

Belligerent: "Come on now. You got it. You know you do. How 'bout it. Mr. Chinese man. Sir. One dollar. Shit. What you need with it?"

"To buy stamps," Tzu says.

"Come on," I say.

The man waves me off, speaks directly to Tzu.

"Just some food is all's I want. I hadn't eat

anything all day. Just wanna get me some corn chips or somethin'. You ain't gonna let a man starve, a brother."

Tzu smiles uncomfortably, says, "I can't give you the dollar."

"Man, you got the money. What you—"

"Come on, Tzu." I slap the man a quarter and pull Tzu away. "You can't talk to these guys; you have to ignore them."

"What you wanna do me that way for?" the man yells. "Don't do me like that."

"Keep walking," I say. "Don't look back."

Tzu does anyway. "Sorry," he calls.

"Sorry, *shit*!" the man yells. "Fuck you, gook. You goddamn gook. You ain't a brother. I'll remember you. I'll remember! Man, we gonna burn your house down!"

The traffic cop on the next corner asks if everything's all right.

The package is from Knoxville, from Liz, my sister. A tin of home-baked Christmas cookies—stars and bells frosted with green and red sugar crystals, snowmen with their heads broken off. I crunch a couple there in the post office lobby, hand a few to Tzu. With his mouth full he asks the clerk for "oversea stamps with an airplane on them." The woman behind him smacks her kid, a wailing knee-baby with corn-rowed hair.

He misses his wife, Tzu says, tearing off a stamp and licking it, aligning it precisely on the rice-paper envelope. He pounds it twice with his fist. People stare.

On our way home, talking this and that, dodging hoi polloi and juking jive-ass dudes with stereos big as bread-boxes hoisted to their shoulders, one of the street crazies—a regular, Anna by name, pasty face, wild gray hair, and teeth like brown corn—waylays us from her home alley. "Kill everybody!" she screams. "Move to New York City and live like a whore! She broke them up and then she killed him!" She glares into Tzu's astounded face. "Sure, I suppose you're Chinese, yeah, not Japanese, no relation, sure, *every*body's Chinese today, well that's no excuse. *Who's going to answer for this,* like they said on the radio, the end of a goddamn era?"

We hurry on. At the crosswalk a kid stands on his stack of *Plain Dealer*s holding the headline turned toward passersby: 'WACKO' KILLS JOHN LENNON.

3

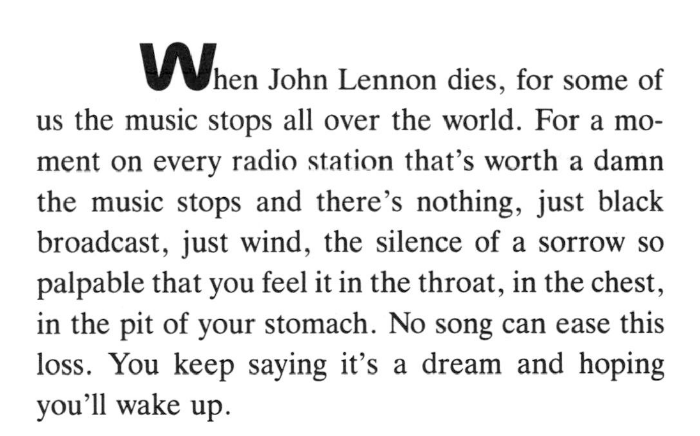

When John Lennon dies, for some of us the music stops all over the world. For a moment on every radio station that's worth a damn the music stops and there's nothing, just black broadcast, just wind, the silence of a sorrow so palpable that you feel it in the throat, in the chest, in the pit of your stomach. No song can ease this loss. You keep saying it's a dream and hoping you'll wake up.

When John Lennon dies people weep openly on the street, they light candles and hold all-night prayer vigils, they stand together in parks, at ball games, on city streets, and join hands and sing "Give Peace a Chance."

When John Lennon dies his voice is everywhere. From apartments and shops and open car windows you can hear "Starting Over," you can hear "Strawberry Fields," "A Day in the Life" and, over and over again, "Imagine." In twenty-four hours every record store in the country sells out the complete Lennon catalog, and people stand mournfully before the display windows where in endless repetition the oversized promo posters for *Double Fantasy* show John kissing Yoko kissing John kissing Yoko kissing John, both with eyes closed, both in black, Yoko wearing a heart pendant, John's fingers in her hair. They kiss too at the newsstands, on page one across from his murderer's mug shot and under a two-deck headline, gracelessly enjambed: JOHN LENNON SHOT/ TO DEATH IN NYC; and there he is, pale and windblown in a new jean jacket and dark sunglasses, on the cover of *Esquire*—JOHN LENNON'S PRIVATE LIFE, a story written before the fact and now out-of-date, late, lost in translation.

When John Lennon dies Suzanne and Chen are curled up on her futon watching *Monday Night Football.* John Lennon, the former Beatle, gunned down in New York City—like ten million other people, Suzanne says bitterly, they hear it first from Howard Cosell.

4

"It was the Patriots and the Dolphins," Chen says. "New England and Miami. For the play-off."

He's standing with Tzu against their bathroom's ratty green wallpaper; from my vantage point (my head and shoulders jammed under the bathroom cabinet) I can only see them from the waist down. Chen has both hands in his jeans pockets. Tzu, a baggy pair of wrinkled wool trousers, wonders aloud for the sixth time if I need any help.

Suzanne is sitting on the edge of the tub, drunk.

"Don't you think it is ironic, Mitchell?" Chen says.

I can't quite get my monkey wrench adjusted around the trap. If I don't get it tightened right, I'll strip the sides of the slip nut. What I need is a pipe wrench. I'm not really up for this.

"You know?" Chen's voice says; he bends and peers into the cabinet. "Because one of John Lennon's albums was called *Revolver*?" Chen says. I grunt. "And he was shot with a revolver?"

"And he'd be alive today if he'd been carrying a gun, right, Chen?" Suzanne says sarcastically.

"Yes, Suzanne," he answers. "I believe he would."

Suzanne says something I can't catch, one word, maybe just an exasperated sound. Late this afternoon, after arguing with Tzu for several hours, Chen and Wa had gone downstairs and bought Little's .38.

"How is it, Mitchell?" Tzu asks.

"Corroded," I say. "It's rust from hell under here." I'm upside down, trying to unscrew clockwise. "Try the other direction?" Tzu says uncertainly.

"I hate that son of a bitch Cosell," Suzanne says, and I can hear her fairy-bell necklace jingling as she speaks. "Of all the bastards on TV"—ah! the nut moves a fraction—"of all the bearers of bad tidings, of all the pompous pricks in the world, why why why did it have to be Howard Cosell? 'A tragedy, sports fans, the famous ex-Beatle John Lennon' "—the wrench slips loose, shit—" 'shot to death on the street. What a loss of potential, what a tragic act of violence.' What a jerk. What does Howard Cosell know about the Beatles. What the fuck does he care?"

"Very sick!" Wa says so suddenly that I jump, and bump my head on the rusty pipe. I didn't know he was here.

"Are you okay?" Tzu asks me.

"America is sick country. Too much money," Wa says, "and more: too much guns. Everybody thinks he is cowboys. And John Lemon, he is from England! John Lemon comes to America and America kills him."

"And that's why you guys bought a gun," I say, sliding out from under the cabinet. Wa stretches his thin lips into a grimacelike smile. The phone rings.

"Give me a break," Suzanne says, looking at the floor; I can't tell if she's talking to me or to Wa.

"About the sink," Tzu says.

I look at each of them in turn: Wa with his smirk, Tzu puzzled, Chen and his bland, blank baby face, Suzanne muting her jingle bell in one fist. They're all four ignoring the phone. "Call the landlord," I say, and nearly knock Wa over on my way out.

5

When she knocks an hour or so later I'm holding a private wake, my own personal retrospective: side one of *Revolver* (yes, Chen, I'll grant you the irony), a few lines into "She Said She Said," with cousin Bob's copies of *Let It Be* and *Rubber Soul* and *Some Time in NYC* all stacked on the changer ready to drop—a Lennon OD. Suzanne stands on my threshold and shakes her head and tells me she isn't coming in until I turn off the music. "I can't bear it," she says. "I can't bear to hear it and I can't bear to not hear it."

I hadn't really seen her in the Chinese bathroom: I was on my back, head under the sink when she and Chen came in, unexpectedly, from wherever they'd been, and they'd caught me by surprise. Now I take a moment to look her over. Backlit by the hall light, her face seems raw and sorrowful—eyes moist and nose red from crying, like someone standing in a cold wind at a funeral. Her hair hangs loose, a little tousled; under her navy blue jacket she wears a baggy charcoal gray sweater and jeans. There's no artifice anywhere about her: just a little eyeliner, a touch of lip gloss, simple hoop earrings, her fairy-bell necklace. In her unadorned right hand (no rings, no nail polish) she holds an unopened bottle of Jim Beam.

"Do you think I'm nuts, Dex?" she says. "To be this distraught?"

I just shrug. She follows me into the kitchen,

where I crack a half-full ice tray into a couple of glasses and pour us each a couple shots of her bourbon.

"I mean, it's not like I'm some aging flower child and the Beatles were my whole life or anything. I was just a kid, you know? I was fifteen, for chrissakes—"

She was fifteen when the Beatles broke up. She was only twelve, a gangly seventh-grader in bobby sox, when the *White Album* came out. She was eight, sprawled on the floor in front of the black-and-white TV, for the *Ed Sullivan* appearance. And it was much the same for me: I'm only a year younger. We never dropped acid to *Sgt. Pepper,* never joined the official fan club or lost our virginity with *Abbey Road* playing in the background, never sang "Give Peace a Chance" at a war protest. But still the music was always there. "We grew up on that music," Suzanne says. "It was like sound-track music for your life. It was always so real, so full of hope and possibility." She shakes her head miserably. "And I loved John, we all loved John. He was the one. You know?" Of course I know. I refill the ice tray. I rip loose a paper towel and wipe at an S-shaped splatter. I look up at the cracked plaster above the fridge, down at a brown stain on the tile floor, and momentarily, inexplicably, hate my life. The ice clatters in her glass. I can't decide if I want her to stay or leave. "They just haven't got a clue," Suzanne says, inclining her head vaguely toward the wall, through which we can hear water running in their kitchen sink—and I know she means Chen, not the other Chinese; that she doesn't expect Wa to care, and Tzu, for all his worldliness, can't really understand, but Chen, somehow, should be able to console her, to mourn with her and comfort her. "Chen knows the Beatles," I say lamely, thinking of our driving lesson; but Suzanne looks at me wonderingly. "You think I'm drunk, don't you?" she says. "I'm not. I'm not drunk, Dex. I've been drinking but I'm perfectly in control. I know what I'm saying."

"Suzanne," I say, "look—"

But she has already turned back to the living room. From the kitchen I watch her bend to the stereo, turn the music all the way down, then back up, then down to just a murmur. She stands in the middle of the white shag carpet, raises both arms over her head, arches her foot and slips off first one shoe, then the other, making a sad little arabesque. In her baggy white cotton socks she hugs herself and croons along with John singing "Across the Universe," throaty and soft and just slightly off-key. I can't stand it. My breath catches and something inside me snaps almost palpably, breaks like the crack of ice, the frozen river swelling, the slow massive floes beginning to move. Looking at Suzanne in her stocking feet, I feel my heart, my numb and bitter heart, melt and yearn, lurch back to life, ache, pound in my throat.

6

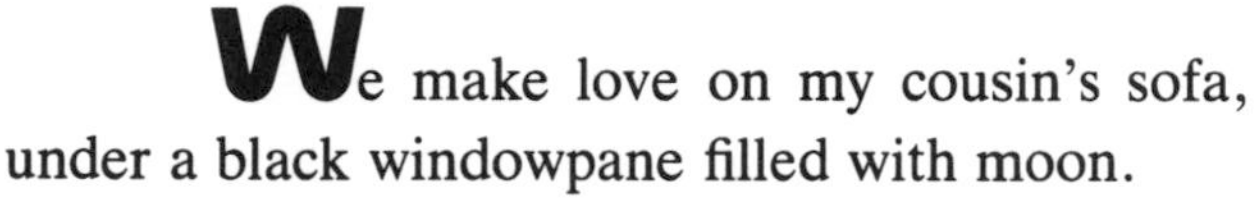

We make love on my cousin's sofa, under a black windowpane filled with moon.

We don't speak at all. It's all breath and hum and sigh but at the end, crying, frantic, our faces wet, she collapses onto me and I'm sure she says into my ear that she loves me. Then I realize I'm saying it too: I love you, Suzanne.

It takes a long time to come back. I feel her heart beating directly over mine. I feel the trickle of sweat between her breasts, pressed against my chest. Her breath is in my ear, against my neck; her hair tickles my face. I trace slow figure eights down the buttons of her spine, I cup her sweet ass and pull. She squeezes me with her thighs. The moon slides behind a cloud. I'm trying to think of the right thing to say. Finally I tell her I can hear our hearts.

She doesn't say anything. Not for the longest time. The record stops. I'm lying there with tears drying on my face, listening to the *psst psst psst* of the stereo, the stylus bumping the ride-out groove. A car door slams outside.

"God," Suzanne says.

I can feel her shaking her head no.

"Don't say anything," she says. "Please? Let's not talk."

Okay. I drift into a nervous half-sleep, where Chen throws open a door to see us making love in a sheet of flames. He burns as he looks at us: his skin crackles and chars, his face melts horribly. I can see inside his rib cage, like a paper lantern filled with bloody light; in the flames his obscenely beating heart blisters and withers like a shriveled apple. At the edge of the dream I hear myself laughing.

I jerk awake, frightened and ashamed. Suzanne, cheek on my shoulder, whispers something I can't catch; she squeezes me and arches her hips just a little so I slide out of her. We're damp everywhere. She rolls off me. "I'm cold, Dex. Could we have a blanket?"

"I'll hold you. I'll keep you warm."

"Could we have a blanket?"

I get up to get the blanket. When I come back she's sitting up, arms locked around legs, chin on her knees, breasts covered, eyes closed. She won't lie back down no matter how I plead. "I think I'd better go," she says. "I've got to work tomorrow"—but I know she's thinking of Chen and what might happen if he finds her car parked out front in the morning.

"What are you going to tell him?" I ask.

"I don't know." She reaches under the couch and fishes out her gray sweater, pulls it on, and then reaches for her jeans.

“If you don’t tell him,” I say—I can’t help it; I try to stop myself but can’t—“if you don’t tell him, I will.”

Suzanne stuffs her panties into her jacket pocket. She slips her shoes on and runs a hand through her tousled hair. Her jingle bell jingles.

“I *will,*” I say miserably.

“No you won’t,” Suzanne says.

7

The man who shot John Lennon was a twenty-five-year-old ex-security guard named Mark David Chapman. For a few days the news is full of him—his love for the Beatles, his three-day stakeout at the Dakota, his over-the-counter, no-questions-asked purchase of a brand new .38-caliber revolver. When the cops came for him he was standing passively a few feet away from Lennon's body, reading a paperback copy of *The*

Catcher in the Rye, a quintessentially American book that I perversely imagine myself recommending to Chen.

I imagine a lot of macabre things over the next two days. I'm not really all there. I can't seem to eat anything, and I sleep in fits, just a few hours at a time, on the couch. When the Chinese knock, I don't answer, though they can hear the stereo and must know I'm home.

I sit at my living room window at dusk and listen to Lennon and watch the buses go by. Twice I see Czapinczyk's black Rabbit circle the block, watching Chen's place for Suzanne, I suppose. I'm in a daze. I finally dial her number, chat a bit as if nothing's amiss, then ask if she'll go with me to the Lennon memorial service at Chester Commons on Sunday. She seems to think a long time before saying that she can't, she needs some space, she wants to be left alone, she can't see anybody now.

Sometime after that—I think it's the next day, but I'm not sure—Tzu knocks. "Mitchell," he calls through the locked door, "I need your help. Please?"

I've seen Tzu in blue since day one. He wears his half-dozen blue shirts all week, one after another six days straight until Sunday mornings, when he dons a dingy tank top or a gray sweatshirt to do laundry. His trousers are blue as well: indigo cotton slacks for warm weather; a navy wool pair, nearly blue-black, for cold. Very carefully he said to me once that he had no "sartorial aspirations," a phrase he'd picked up God knows where—at some staid faculty function, perhaps, or thumbing through an old *GQ* in an international airport lounge somewhere. Blue shirts were efficient: "I never have to decide what color to wear," he'd said. So I'm almost speechless now to see him out of uniform, standing at my door in a gray-on-white pinstripe button-down with a red-and-black paisley tie knotted misshapenly at the collar. He has brushed his thick hair back and it stands stiffly up, held in place by some fragrant Chinese pomade. Except for his clunky shoes, he looks like any

M.B.A. on the way to a job interview. He looks corporate.

I stare. I stutter, start to ask what's gotten into him, but he cuts me off: "I am going today to an important appointment. And . . . so . . ."

He's staring back at me. I realize it's been two days since I've looked in a mirror—my hair must be wild—and I'm standing barefoot at the door, bare-chested with my maroon robe hanging open, dirty sweatpants sagging low on my hips. Tzu doesn't know where to look. So he looks away, his brown sorrowful eyes darting around the wrecked living room: sofa pillows scattered helter-skelter, a half-full bowl of soup on the floor, my red jockey shorts draped across the coffee table, a single whiskey glass tipped sideways in a brown puddle on the carpet. Tzu's sad face gets sadder. I wonder, disgusted with myself, whether he's ever made love on a sofa, drunk. I wonder whether he and his wife were virgins when they got married.

"Ah, Mitchell," he says, as if his heart is breaking.

I try to help him with the tie. I stand behind

him, arms around him as we peer into the hallway mirror. "Relax your shoulders," I murmur—I can't get my arms around. I start to show him: skinny side here, cross the fat side over, now you try it— "Please," he says, almost exasperated. He doesn't have time to learn this today, and besides, he's not sure he'll ever need to know it again. So I work in silence; I have to start over twice, peering around his stiff shoulders into the mirror, and for the first time I notice at the back of his head a dime-sized bald spot and realize with a shock that Tzu is even older than I thought—thirty-five? Older?

He's going to the police, he says, after straightening the tie and thanking me formally. Why? I ask. He perhaps shouldn't say, he says. Then apologizes: "Mitchell, I am sorry to mention it. I can see you are upset. But I think that perhaps Suzanne has been here? And though you may think it is none of my business, I will say that she has brought only trouble on us all."

"She's not a bad person, Tzu," I start to say.

"Do you know why I am meeting the police?" He actually waits for me to shake my head. "It is because of Suzanne. She has told this man, this Mick Czapinczyk, that she is dating Chen, sleeping with him. And he was her old boyfriend. So now he calls our house. All the time, at any hour, and threatens Mr. Chen." He's told Chen horrible things, Tzu says furiously, too horrible to repeat. Things like how he has black men who work for him and how they're always watching Chen and how they'll cut Chen with razor blades. And maybe some white men who work for him too. Or maybe he himself. And worse things, things about Suzanne, things about Suzanne and Chen in bed. Tzu says sometimes Mick talks so fast they can't understand him; it's gotten so they're all three afraid to answer the phone. "This is the reason we have bought the gun." Mick himself suggested it. " 'You better get a gun, gook,' " Tzu says he said. " 'You're gonna need it.' " Tzu shakes his head violently. "I will not have it," he says. "But Chen has lost his mind from fear, and Mr. Wa also wanted the gun, to protect us." Wa was in the Red Guard, or something, and knows how to shoot. Tzu shudders. "I could not convince them. They voted."

"Democracy in action," I mumble.

"Stupidity in action," Tzu says, dead serious. "And it is all from Suzanne. If Chen had never met her . . ."

"Listen, Tzu," I say, "Forget the cops. You don't need the cops. I'll take care of everything. I'll call Zap this afternoon and talk some sense into him; I'll get him to leave Chen alone, and you can give Little his gun back."

His face brightens. "Will you do this?" he asks. "If you can do this, and we can avoid the police . . ."

To hell with the police, I tell him; the police couldn't do anything anyway. As for Suzanne, she's not what he thinks. "Don't hate her, Tzu. She has a good heart. She's just confused. She needs some space." I tell him what she told me: she just wants to be left alone. I'm babbling. I gesture stupidly toward the disheveled couch, as if that explains everything. "She's not in love with Chen," I say. "That's over with. So don't worry about it."

"Oh, Mitchell, my friend," Tzu says. His eyes soften and he looks at me with something more than affection—something, I think, like pity. He puts one hand to his tie, tugs at the knot in agony. "He is with her right now. Still. Since seven-thirty last night."

Later that day—a long time later, after I've tried my damnedest to stop thinking entirely, and failed—I go downstairs to talk to Monty.

五

Long shot: Chen, back to camera, standing in Sears before a wall of color televisions. From this distance we can't tell what the screens show; we can only see that the sets are turned to the same channel: the images are identical, and they swirl and jump in unison as if the wall is alive, some giant colorful amoeba. A salesman approaches, asks Chen something; he shakes his head no, and keeps watching. After a moment more, he turns toward the camera, smiles, and walks forward. He goes out of focus for a second.

ANTIGONE

(*v.o.*)

We're conducting a survey. What's your favorite TV show?

CUT TO

A series of quick "man-in-the-street"-type interviews, various settings, people apparently selected at random.

MAN IN RED JACKET

No contest! *Monday Night Football.*

BLOND WOMAN

Lou Grant. Great show. Realistic, you know?

LADY WITH BABY

Dallas, I guess. I like that Larry Hagman. I used to never miss an *I Dream of Jeannie,* can you believe that? I'm a real fan.

MAN WITH GROCERIES

Three's Company? I dunno. You tell me.

KIMI HU

I don't watch it. Who has time to watch it? It's totally stupid.

ANTIGONE

(*v.o.*)

You don't even watch soaps?

KIMI HU

(*guilty*)

Oh, well! Soaps, yeah, well, I guess I was thinking about prime-time TV. Yeah, I'm a soap addict. *As the World Turns* and *The*

Young and the Restless. And I was like on a *General Hospital* kick for a while, too.

ANTIGONE

(*v.o.*)

What's your favorite TV show?

BILLY OWENS

(*doing his two-second Hitchcock cameo*) *Championship Wrestling.*

MAILMAN

Star Trek reruns.

ANTIGONE'S MOTHER

The Jeffersons! Best show on TV.

CUT TO

A series of quick cuts: black people, white people, women, men, kids, each one saying, with varying degrees of enthusiasm, The Jeffersons*! The last shot of this series shows a young white boy, maybe* *five years old, twirling and bopping, clapping his hands rhythmically and singing, with a slight lisp, the theme from* The Jeffersons*: "Movin' On Up."*

CUT TO

Medium shot: Elizabeth Shapiro, associate professor of Media Studies, sitting against a wall of books in her office. She's white, middle-aged, with iron gray streaks through her short dark hair. She stares intently into the camera as she speaks. Sync-sound.

SHAPIRO

(*v.o.*)

It's a global medium now. It's not really an American form anymore. It's an international medium, with the power to break down linguistic and cultural barriers. TV is postverbal; it's image-driven, and it's a global signifier. It has significance to everyone.

CUT TO

Another montage of television images, this one apparently randomly edited, just continuous jump cuts: politicians gesturing, aspirin commercials, a news anchor smiling, a white woman driving a red convertible, a black man in handcuffs, images flashing faster and faster, building chaotically until the cuts are too quick to follow.

SHAPIRO

(*v.o.*)

Almost everything that's said about television today is simply too facile. It's this, it's that. I don't think it's possible nowadays to watch TV without a theory of TV. Otherwise there's no context. You're awash in these images, these distorted, recycled mythologies, without any anchor, any way of interpreting. Without a theory, it's just a lot of white noise.

ANTIGONE

(*v.o.*)

What do you mean, a theory?

CUT TO

Shapiro, smiling. During the next speech, she is repeatedly interrupted by loud bursts of static and TV snow, each interruption a bit longer.

SHAPIRO

For instance, I myself am a poststructuralist feminist critic. (*Static.*) Clearly, in order to properly view TV in a cultural context, you need to be solidly grounded in theory. (*Static.*) . . . crucial to note that TV is first of all an ideological matrix, it's a medium of (*Static.*) . . . postmodern, antistructuralist approach. (*Static.*) . . . misreading of Lévi-Strauss (*Static.*) . . . deconstruct the text of TV.

Four or five seconds of snow and static. The film seems to be self-destructing. Then a short glimpse of Shapiro nodding at the camera, with Antigone's uncertain voice-over asking "ideological subtext?" Then another burst of static.

CUT TO

Chen in Sears. He is standing in front of a video camera; behind him a display TV hooked to the camera shows his live image: Chen on TV! He looks at us over his shoulder, grinning, then looks back to the TV; he waves to himself and his image instantaneously waves back.

FREEZE FRAME:

Chen waving, grinning. Five-second pause.

CUT TO VIDEO SNOW, WHITE NOISE

CUT TO BLACK

1

Driving across town to the John Lennon memorial service Sunday afternoon, with Chen somberly chewing his nails beside her and another terrible Beatles tribute issuing from her car radio, Suzanne runs over a squirrel. She sees it coming; she swerves, brakes, but can't stop, and the poor stupid thing dives directly under her front tire. Suzanne pulls over, flicks on her hazard blinkers, and flings open her door. She stands helplessly in the weave of traffic—people honking and cursing—and watches the broken bundle of blood and fur flop and twitch a few quick seconds; and I can imagine her there in her open camel-hair coat, face contorted, whispering over and over *I'm sorry I'm sorry I'm sorry.* Not your fault, Chen says, touching her shoulder from behind, and she tells him it was her fault, and he says *not*—but if they say anything else, she doesn't remember it later.

What she does remember is an ominous feeling, almost a foreboding, as if the oddly bright December sun had suddenly slipped behind a cloud, as if Chen's face shone somehow tragic and doomed. Perhaps that's hindsight, Suzanne looking back afterwards in grief, trying to connect, to understand, to see what was coming. Whatever: there's an undercurrent of something between them, she feels later, a sense of veiled meaning under their simple words, of things slipping out of alignment, of shapes just out of sight rising slowly to the surface.

They're late for the service. One thing about

Cleveland: we take our rock and roll seriously in this town. Chester Commons is a sad sea of blue-jeaned folk—fans, freaks, rockers, geeks, preppies, and ex-hippies, teary-eyed high school girls, boys holding flowers, moms and dads with kids too young to understand, curious homeless and a wandering guitarist or two—maybe ten thousand people all told; and as Suzanne and Chen thread their way through the knots of mourners, she becomes aware of his constant quick searching glances to each side and his too-tight grip on her hand; she stops walking and turns questioningly to him: What's wrong with you? Chen bites his lip. Fine, he says. Fine. No problem. He won't meet her eyes. His upper lip seems to tremble. And Suzanne realizes then that he's terrified—surrounded by thousands of weeping, emotional, violent Americans, whose bulky jackets and deep-pocketed overcoats must surely conceal guns, knives, and God knows what else—and though she understands his fear, she also instantly despises it. ("It was disgusting to me," she said later, "it was pathetic. *He* was pathetic.") Why in hell did she bring him? she wonders. She lets go of his hand and angrily kicks a pinecone.

Someone onstage is going on and on about Lennon and his dream, and how the dream hasn't died, and we all have to carry on. Someone from the mayor's office harangues for fifteen minutes about handgun laws. A minor rock star with permed hair and artfully torn jeans holds forth about the first time he heard the Beatles and how it changed his life forever, and two local deejays do the same, and finally there's ten whole minutes of silence for John—nothing but birdsong and traffic and an occasional baby crying. Then everyone starts singing "Give Peace a Chance," and it's too much for Suzanne. She begins to weep, steadily, brokenly, singing through her tears and scanning the crowd in vain for a friendly face, and when Chen reaches out to stroke her hair, she jerks back without thinking and knocks his hand away.

On the way home they hardly speak. She feels old, and at a stoplight, examining her red-rimmed eyes in the rearview mirror, she suddenly notices Mick Czapinczyk's black Rabbit two cars back, a Christmas tree incongruously bound to the roof, tied with bright yellow cord. "Goddamn son of a *bitch!*" Suzanne cries, and Chen twists around in his seat to look. They hang a right. So does Zap. Suzanne floors it. Same thing. Furious, she pulls over. "I was going to have it out with him," she said to me later, "get it over with, once and for all. That lunatic. I was sick of him following me around, threatening me. I'd had it."

There's no way to recount what happens next without crossing into melodrama. Chen panics, begs Suzanne to keep driving. She won't. He pulls Little's thirty-eight from his jacket, saying hysterically that he's ready for Zap and his black boys, that he knows how to protect himself. He's speaking so fast that spit flies from his lips. He'll kill them all, he says. In the middle of this, Czapinczyk cruises by, honks, waves gaily, and keeps going.

Suzanne is livid. And terrified. "I thought I was going to pass out. It was a nightmare. I *hate* guns. Jesus Christ." She screams at Chen to get out, that she's not driving another inch with a gun in her car. He pleads with her to take him to her house, to hide him from Czapinczyk. "We were both shaking, Dex. We were screaming at each other like crazy people. It was all I could do to keep from hitting him, I was so scared and mad." She threatens to get out and walk. He says he's keeping the pistol. Finally, a little calmer, they compromise: he'll unload it if she'll drive. Okay. She watches, horrified, as he breaks open the chamber and dumps out the cartridges. "Here," she says, reaching for them, but Chen drops them in his shirt pocket. She stares at him a long moment, searching his haggard face for something recognizable; she's trying to decide what she ought to do. Chen can't bear her gaze. He turns away in anguish, sighs something in Chinese. "That was all it took. Somehow it was like a wall coming down, cutting me off." She throws the Z into gear and announces she's taking him home. No reaction. They drive a block or two in silence, with Chen looking distantly out the window. This is the hard part. She hears herself telling him she thinks they should stop seeing each other. "I can't do this, Chen," she says slowly. "I just can't take this. I don't know who you are anymore. This is crazy. It's over. Please."

Chen begins to cry. He slaps the empty pistol against his thigh rhythmically. "It is because of Mitchell," he says, choking back tears. "I know. Tzu have told me."

"Told you what?" Suzanne asks sickly, but Chen won't say. "It has nothing to do with Mitchell," Suzanne insists, but she can't convince him, and finally she gives up, tells him to believe whatever he wants.

When they pull up to our building in the dim afternoon, Zap's Christmas tree is a flaming torch scorching the sidewalk.

December, that most difficult, hectic, materialistic month of the Christian industrial world calendar, has finally and powerfully exerted its capitalistic pull on me: I go shopping. Christmas shopping, on a mid-December Sunday, which is to say, I've lost my mind. Worse, I go by myself. What is more lonely than solo Christmas shopping? Everywhere you look are lovers, families, friends and neighbors in couples and troikas and gaggles and herds, and if by chance you ever spot some other solitary soul, you can bet it's only temporary: someone who's sneaked away from the gang to pursue a secret gift. And how hatefully cheery are the piped-in Christmas carols!

I'm out of my element here. I've driven forty-five minutes deep into the suburbs, light-years from my squalid midtown neighborhood, to a gleaming triple-deck mall, and for a while I just wander the wide spaces, stunned by the neat displays of pricey stuff, the visual overload, the even and steady roar of people consuming. I fend off salesfolk. I jostle through hordes. I suavely try to catch the eye of a sleek woman in jeans and black boots, but she's on automatic pilot, mesmerized by half-price leather luggage.

So why fight it? I blow a bitter kiss to a red-haired mannequin (yes, red like Suzanne's, but short and kinky) and then shift into shopping mode. I go nuts with the plastic. Visa, MasterCard, Sears, Penney's. I start with Mom and Dad. A nightgown, a velour robe. Next: Billy and Antigone: a book on Hitchcock (read something, dammit!), a pair of faux-ivory earrings. Then a silk blouse for my sis. I'm gathering everyone in my life into these ever-accumulating and increasingly heavy shopping bags. I mentally run down my list. Cortez and Monty get new mittens, and I grab a six-pack of Australian lager for Little. That leaves the Chinese. And Suzanne, of course. Which is how I end up in Intimate Apparel downstairs in Marshall's, and that's where I meet Tia, a fetchingly long-legged salesclerk in black spike heels, who has that certain easy, straightforward flirtatiousness peculiar to very tall women. Tia is at least five-eleven, with a quick smile and enormous brown eyes, and on this, her first day as temp sales help, the old bats who lorded over the bras and panties and French-cut bikinis hadn't bothered to teach her the cash register; instead, they shoved her out of the way and told her to just look busy, get out on the floor and wander. When she asks me if I need any help, and our eyes lock (levelly, at exactly the same height), I pull my hand out of a dump-table pile of brassieres and smile. She smiles back. We smile a little more, and then she amends her opening with, "Or are you just wandering around feeling the lace?" I make some goofy response about being caught red-handed, and then I take a deep breath as she and I hop on our own personal roller coaster, strap ourselves in and start climbing; and though there's a slow steep slope to get up, the other side promises dizzy downhills and flat-out giddiness. I ask her why lingerie departments are invariably staffed by matronly granny types, and whether there's some law against hiring attractive, shapely young women to sell underwear; and Tia says mock-seriously that beautiful young clerks would embarrass the men who came in to buy for their wives and girlfriends, and asks which one I'm buying for; and I grin slyly and shrug and tell her . . . but why embarrass myself? Suffice it to say that when she clocks out forty-five minutes later we go for a glass of wine at her apartment nearby, where after a while one thing leads to another and we end up half-undressed rolling around on her black velvet couch together; and in the lambent light of her TV during a slow swoop on the roller-coaster ride

I establish that Tia does indeed have exquisite taste in intimate apparel (though the apparel stays on and the hands stay outside). We kiss and nuzzle and pinch and tickle, and giggle a bit, and bite and gurgle, and for a few hours I'm happy, I forget Suzanne and Chen and Czapinczyk and everything else—my whole goddamn life, in other words—until I ask for her phone number on my way out and Tia, standing in her doorway in her disarrayed burgundy camisole, brings that roller-coaster car to a dead lurching halt (Ride over! Everybody out!) by wondering aloud whether or not that's a good idea, because she's "sorta seeing somebody" who'll probably be back in town "tomorrow or the day after."

So! I walk like a zombie back to my Christmas-crammed car, feeling evil and put-out. This is surely some kind of cosmic joke, and in the morning, after eight hours of sleep and a hefty breakfast, I'll get the punch line. At the moment, though, I'm having trouble laughing. I drive home through a misty 2:00 A.M. fog, punching absently at the radio buttons to avoid the occasional (still!)

Lennon death oratory. I'm exhausted, too worn out to give a damn about anything at all. Staggering up our sidewalk like some skinny Santa Claus, fishing for my keys with an armload of bags, I sniff gasoline—what the hell?—and nearly trip over the charred remnants of Czapinczyk's Christmas tree. The only lit window in the building is Chen's, and looking up at that warm rectangle of light I half expect to see his smug silhouette. It's 2:30 A.M. on the last day of his life.

3

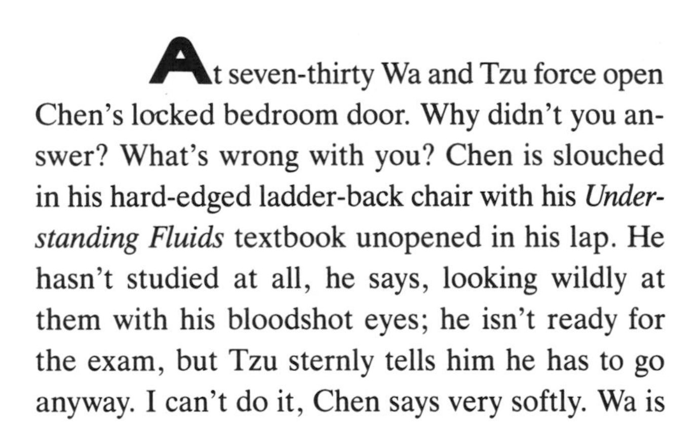

At seven-thirty Wa and Tzu force open Chen's locked bedroom door. Why didn't you answer? What's wrong with you? Chen is slouched in his hard-edged ladder-back chair with his *Understanding Fluids* textbook unopened in his lap. He hasn't studied at all, he says, looking wildly at them with his bloodshot eyes; he isn't ready for the exam, but Tzu sternly tells him he has to go anyway. I can't do it, Chen says very softly. Wa is outraged. Chen is a discredit to his country and a shameful son to his parents. I don't care, Chen sighs, and as Wa rants—Idiot! What do you mean, you don't care? Have you lost your mind?—Tzu crouches, takes Chen by the shoulders, and tells him that they love him. You must do this for us, Chen, he says. If you fail, we all fail.

On the way to campus, they walk a few yards behind Wa so they can talk. Mostly Tzu just listens, sick with worry. Chen keeps trailing off in midsentence, oblivious. He can't stop thinking of her. He has never known such pain. And with Mitchell right next door—how can he continue to live in the same building? He wishes he'd never come here, and he's going back to China as soon as exams are over. They cross a street against a red light, weaving through the traffic; Chen doesn't even glance up. Don't be so rash, Tzu remembers telling him. Listen: you must make your peace with Suzanne and Mitchell.

They get to class a few minutes after eight, late for the first time all semester. Chen takes the exam and bombs it badly. At lunch he stares into his untouched noodle soup and says, I did not complete a single question. Wa hisses. Tzu tells him it's not important, and that he must go speak with Mitchell.

He tries. For almost ten minutes that afternoon, from 3:14 to 3:23 on my digital clock, he taps softly at my front door, repeating the same pattern: a hesitant double triplet, a long pause, then another knock. He knows I'm home—my car's out front and the TV's on. He knocks louder, listens longer, calls my name a few times. He can't hear me when I tell him under my breath to fuck off. Sneaky bastard.

At 3:24 the phone rings. "Mitchell," he says.

We listen to each other breathing. In the background I can hear the telephonic murmur of their TV from their living room.

"I'm sorry, Mitchell," he says. "Forgive me please. I never knew she was your girlfriend."

"She wasn't," I say, "she's not."

He seems confused. "But Zap said—" He coughs, starts over. "She and you were lovers? You love each other?"

"What do you want, Chen?"

"I want to know this."

"Why? It's none of your business."

"No," he says sadly, but I don't know whether he's agreeing or arguing. I tell him I don't have anything to say to him and that I'm hanging up now.

"Mitchell," he says, "my friend. We are friends. You helped me at the hospital, in the emergency room. You teach me to drive. You were always kind to me. So why won't you tell me this, if she was your girlfriend?"

"Because," I say.

"Because?"

I consider various answers. I'm so tired. My head is spinning. "Chen, that's something you should ask her. It's between the two of you. Just leave me out of it, okay? And besides, what the hell do you care?" (Because, see, I had no idea. I thought they were still together.)

"I don't know anymore who to believe," Chen says, almost to himself.

"Ask her," I say. "Call her right now and ask."

"I am afraid to do it."

"Suit yourself," I say, and hang up.

Only a few weeks before, he would have seized happily upon that "suit yourself," another new idiom for his collection of odd English.

4

He calls her at work. She won't talk. He insists. At last, weary to death of the whole thing, she tells him what he wants to know: how we'd gone out a few times, how we were lovers, how we'd been together Tuesday night—not trying to hurt him but thinking that at least he'd leave her alone now.

When he finally hangs up the phone, the last blushes of sunset still color the Chinese windowpanes. I imagine him standing at his bedroom window a moment looking out, wondering what had gone wrong, maybe fixing one last image of Suzanne in his memory, maybe hating me. Maybe nothing. Wa said later that he thought he heard sobs from Chen's room but he wasn't sure.

He's wearing his Salvation Army gray wool sweater over a white poly-cotton button-down, suede snow boots with red laces, and his beloved blue jeans. He wanders down the hall and stands, abstracted, both hands in his pockets, in the living room, where Wa, in an uncharacteristically compassionate mood, tries to cheer him up and Chen keeps shaking his head and smiling. He pulls his goose-down vest from the hall closet, then sleepwalks back to his room for the pistol, which he slips into his right-hand vest pocket. Wa asks again what's wrong as Chen drifts through the living room, and he turns at the door and says, in Chinese, "Nothing. I'm going for a walk."

He opens their door and from my own living room, where I'm lying on the couch flipping stupidly through the new *American Film,* I can hear Wa yell. I drop my magazine on the floor and roll over on my side, listening. Chen says something, four or five words, then stands a moment on the landing before he shuts the door. Outside, a cop car blows by with its siren howling, chased by an ambulance. Some kids on bikes cruise past, yelling *Death to the invaders* and making outer space explosions and loud laser noises. Then silence. Nothing else seems to move as Chen descends the first step. Right then I'm trying to decide whether I hate him or Suzanne more. Right then Monty Little is crouched at the bottom of the stairs jabbering secret incantations over a bundle of twigs. And right then, three blocks away at a red light, Mick Czapinczyk is sitting in his black VW Rabbit, on his way to Chen's apartment.

5

Everything else we piece together afterwards in the DA's office.

At the bottom of the stairs he is waylaid by Monty, who stands and spreads his arms wide with fingers curled like claws. "You cannot pass," Monty chants, and then he screams, "You cannot pass, Chinese man!"

Chen sits down on the stairs. He just looks at Monty, who begins ego-tripping, intoning a spell in a tremendous voice, like God speaking out of his tiny body. "I am the great Montezuma Little. My name is Little but I am big. I am big as a mountain. I am all-powerful. I talk on the radio. I get on TV and destroy people's minds. I suck your mama's titty. I put a spell on you that will make you shake and puke and pee blood."

Chen tells him to get out of the way.

"I will not move for no Chinese man."

Chen says something about telling Monty's dad.

"He ain't home. He ain't talking to you."

Chen says that he'll kill Monty if he doesn't move. ("He did," Monty said later. "He did too say it.") He draws the pistol and holds it up just out of Monty's reach, and laughs horribly. Czapinczyk pulls up across the street and gets out of his car.

"That ain't yours," Monty says, and he grabs at the gun. "Hey, that ain't yours. That's my dad's. You better give it back."

"Let me pass," Chen says, loud enough for me to hear.

Monty spreads his arms again. "You gimme that gun and you can go. Or if you don't, I'mon put a hurtin' spell on you."

Czapinczyk starts up the sidewalk.

"Gimme my dad's gun. You gimme."

Chen does. He hands it to Monty with the safety off, and then stands up. He opens his jacket and tells Monty to shoot. "Here." He points to his heart.

Monty backs up, points the pistol at Chen. "You crazy. Get offa me. Naw. Get."

Czapinczyk's hand is on the doorknob.

Chen takes one step toward Monty. And then as Zap pushes open the door, Chen calls Monty a name. "Chapman," he says. "Shoot me, Mark David Chapman."

Upstairs I stand and start for the door, too late. For one instant Mick Czapinczyk looms in the threshold in his Ninth Street Cinema 3-D glasses, blinking, trying to adjust to the darkness. Nobody moves. Then in a fury of hatred Chen throws himself at Zap, and Monty, standing between them clutching his father's gun, Monty, unprotected by all his black magic, poor Monty screams as all three of them crash to the floor and the gun goes off.

6

They took our statements separately. I sat across from a gray-faced Little, who held Monty on his lap, stroking his hair and murmuring to him soothingly. (Cortez, easily bored, had repaired to the coffee room, where he begged quarters from hookers and car thieves and idly kicked dents in the grubby out-of-order drink machine. Later I overheard him boasting to a freckle-faced white kid that his brother Montezuma was on trial for "murder with a deadly weapon.") There was no good-cop, bad-cop routine, no film-noir blinding light in the face, just a stenographer and two laconic homicide detectives going through the motions. They grilled Czapinczyk, though, who irked them by refusing to remove his bloody fatigue jacket; and after Suzanne and her lawyer had given her statement, they grilled him again; and then Tzu and Wa, accompanied by the university attorney and the associate dean of student affairs, spent almost an hour telling their side. Finally they had us each back for a follow-up, and then the assistant DA was called in and got the story and talked to us one at a time. He couldn't figure out whom to charge, he said; it looked to him like the shooting should be ruled accidental. There'd be a hearing sometime in January. Monty would probably be put on two years' probation. Little might be charged with illegal sale of a firearm, though no money had actually changed hands (the Chinese had been between stipend checks). Michael Allen Czapinczyk was to immediately cease and desist any and all harassment of involved parties, but especially Suzanne. Nobody was to leave town until after the hearing.

In the dark parking lot, with Tzu clutching his arm, Wa cursed me bitterly in vile Chinese, face contorted behind his tear-fogged glasses.

7

After Chen's death, Billy Owens brooded for weeks, kicking himself, eaten up by hindsight. He'd made the wrong movie. His lifelong aesthetic mission, as he used to call it, was to purge cinema of its decadent narrative element; concepts and images should always take precedent over story—but in Chen's American life and death there was a story not even Billy could ignore. He spent hours going over his footage, revising, rethinking the whole film. For once he had hit upon a tale that needed telling—love, death, corrupted innocence—and he had no way to tell it. There wasn't enough of the right sort of footage. The shots were wrong, he said. All in all, he had four hours thirty-seven minutes of Chen—but it was mostly about TV, useless now. He spent a few days erasing sound tracks and splicing together a lot of silent Chen footage, and he wrote some expository voice-overs for Antigone, hoping to tell the story that way, but the effect was unbearably hokey, strained and contrived. He asked Wa and Tzu to sit for new interviews, "as a memorial to Chen," he told them, but they weren't buying. He kept after them until Tzu—gentle, gracious Tzu—threatened to smash Billy's face. Undaunted, Billy pressed on elsewhere, with the ghoulish intensity of a TV reporter covering a disaster: interviewing Little in the front yard, tracking Czapinczyk around town, hounding Suzanne until Antigone finally declared *Enough!* and called him off, saying he'd sunk lower than a snake's belly and she was ashamed to be his fiancée. He moped awhile, then shot a lot more footage—backtracking, circling, looking for some thread of continuity, anything. He asked the director of international studies if any other students had been shot to death ("Not to our knowledge"). He filmed a ten-minute bit with the autopsy M.D., who explained in precise detail how the bullet had entered between the sixth and seventh ribs, punctured the left lung and ruptured the aorta before glancing off the right scapula on the way out; Chen had almost certainly died instantly. He interviewed the mortician, who detailed the procedure for airline shipment (a plywood crate and foam padding around a sealed coffin). He got a few lines from the responding officers and searched half-heartedly for the ambulance crew, but by then he'd realized that everything he was doing was surface, not content; that while he might be able to document all the facts, interview all the friends and family and every single person involved, he'd still only be filming *around* this death; he'd never understand it, no one would, really; and so in despair, he gave up. He went back to his original concept of the Chinese as commentators on America-cum-TV, building and reshaping and editing as a kind of denial: he completely ignored Chen's death, made no reference to it in the final cut.

Which made it an achingly difficult film to watch. From the black background Chen's dead face peers out, animated and brightly hopeful. He smiles and waves from the front seat of my car. He sits in tears before the TV, giggling helplessly at Bugs Bunny. He mails his weekly Cleveland picture postcard to his lonely mother. He struggles ludicrously with a Big Mac. "I must eat it for my Chinese friends," he says between bites. "When I return home, they will have a thousand questions. They will want to know everything about America." Antigone asks what he'll say about the hamburger. Chen laughs, delighted: "More research necessary!" My heart broke, watching him, and I was racked with guilt and remorse. I had no idea whether it was a good movie or not—how could I be objective?—but I wasn't surprised when Billy never got a distribution deal. "It's in the can," he said, after trying one last reedit, "and it's gonna stay in the can." He and Antigone used what was left of their arts council grant to start a new picture, a comic documentary on the absurd expense of American weddings, starring Billy and Antigone themselves. The last time I saw *Watching TV with the Red Chinese* was in early March, at thc Johnsons' annual film party, projected like some sad home movie on their freshly painted plaster wall.

8

Suzanne left town in February. An old college roommate had an extra bedroom in L.A., and Cleveland held no promise for her anymore, only obsessive memories of Chen, her busted marriage, Czapinczyk. She needed a change of scene, big-time, she told me. "Christ, Dex, what a year I've had," she said wearily, pressing her palms to both temples. I must have really loved her, or maybe been moved by some kind of morbid curiosity, because for a couple of nights after the inquest I stayed with her and held her while she told me the whole story. "It's my fault," she sobbed. "I feel like I'm responsible. I killed him." "No," I whispered, "*I* did"—but she must have thought I was just being kind, trying to ease her burden; all she said was "Oh, Dex." We didn't make love; we didn't even kiss. I don't know what I was hoping for. It was hard to be there those few nights, and even harder to let her go. The last time I saw her, she was sitting cross-legged on her living room carpet, boxing up her few books for the big move, and she'd had her lovely long hair cropped short all over, California punk–style.

Chen's death was ruled accidental, which would have amused him no end. He believed that there are no accidents, no fortuitous events, that God (whatever that means) does not play at dice. Everything is connected, he'd said, each event is a matrix of force and energy, and the architecture of sequential moments in space-time is immutable. The sparrow falls, the plane is missed, the car runs out of gas on the railroad tracks: timing is all.

I keep thinking: if Czapinczyk had caught two more red lights, he'd have missed Chen entirely. If Suzanne had hung up a few minutes earlier, Chen would have been off the phone and out the door that much sooner. If Monty had gone inside when his daddy had called him, he'd have been washing up for supper as Chen came downstairs. And how far back could you take it? If John Lennon hadn't been murdered. If Suzanne hadn't dated Czapinczyk. If Chen had never gone to the Halloween party. An infinite number of *if*s, any one of which could have thrown awry this particular convergence of choice and motion, rearranged this tableau of Chen and Monty and Czapinczyk sprawled on the landing, blood seeping into our dingy brown carpet.

Think about this long enough, with enough guilt, and you begin to see the attraction of Czapinczyk's philosophy. In another possible world, Chen leaves the gun in his pocket instead of handing it to Monty. In some other possible world he carries it unloaded. In another he carries a knife, not a gun. Everything else is exactly the same:

Suzanne, me, Czapinczyk. The permutations are endless: In another possible world he never comes to America; he flunks his English refresher course, or studies poetry instead of calculus, or becomes a Chinese acrobat. In another possible world he lives in a dorm room on campus; he never meets Suzanne, and she and I live happily ever after with no Chinese. There is even in this infinite realm a possible world where no Chinese exist at all—no Chen, no Wa, no Tzu, no Mao Tse-tung, no Confucius, no Kubla Khan, no Charlie Chan. In another possible world, Chen is Greek. In another possible world, Chen's a girl.

In another possible world, I'm absolved: I never tell Monty to leave Wa alone, to curse Chen instead.

But these are fantasies, linguistic chimeras contrived so we can understand that most human of all ideas: the yearning for things to be other than they are. They take up delicate mental airspace, these worlds: they're imaginary castles built on clouds, more ephemeral than soap bubbles. In the end they mean nothing. We're able to acknowledge these infinities, to consider them, but in the last analysis we're doomed, I understand now, to live and act and interpret here, in this, the best of all possible worlds.